THE
ADVENTURES
OF
RANALD
BANNERMAN

THE
ADVENTURES
OF
RANALD
BANNERMAN

GEORGE MACDONALD

BETHANY HOUSE PUBLISHERS
MINNEAPOLIS, MINNESOTA 55438

Ranald Bannerman's Boyhood was first published in 1871
by Strahan & Co. , London.

Cover illustration by Dan Thornberg,
Bethany House Publishers staff artist.

Published by Bethany House Publishers
A Ministry of Bethany Fellowship, Inc.
6820 Auto Club Road, Minneapolis, Minnesota 55438

Printed in the United States of America

Library of Congress Cataloging-in-Publication Data

MacDonald, George, 1824–1905.
    The adventures of Ranald Bannerman / George MacDonald ; edited by
Michael R. Phillips.
        p. cm. — (George MacDonald classics for young readers)
    Rev. ed. of: Ranald Bannerman's boyhood.
    Summary: A young Scottish boy relates his adventures growing up with
his three brothers in a small country town in northern Scotland, where
their father is a clergyman.

    [1. Brothers—Fiction. 2. Country life—Fiction.
3. Scotland—Fiction. 4. Christian life—Fiction.]
I. Phillips, Michael R. , 1946– . II. MacDonald, George, 1824–1905.
Ranald Bannerman's boyhood. III. Title. IV. Series.
PZ7.M1475Ad   1991
[Fic]—dc20   91–25639
ISBN 1–55661–223–0   CIP
                                                AC

Contents

INTRODUCTION

G eorge MacDonald's most famous and best-selling book was
released to the public in 1871. It was, of course, *At the Back of
the North Wind*, which you may already have read as part of this
Bethany House Series of George MacDonald's books.

But the very fame and popularity and attention received by
North Wind kept many of George MacDonald's readers at the time
from noticing another book that he wrote the same year. In fact,
MacDonald wrote only those two books in 1871: one his *most* well-
known title; the other, one of his *least*. That isn't to say both weren't
good, maybe even equally good. But with all the attention focused
on Diamond's story, there just wasn't much left to go around for
the story of the other boy MacDonald wrote about that year.

The 1871 companion release to *At the Back of the North Wind* is
the book you are holding in your hand, which was first called *Ranald
Bannerman's Boyhood*.

As an author, George MacDonald often wrote about himself,
though he disguised his own thoughts and feelings and experiences
by putting them into the lives of his fictional characters. Then he
mixed in all sorts of made-up incidents in order to create a story,
so you can hardly tell what actually happened to MacDonald and
which things are pure fiction. This is an especially good example
of what we might call "autobiographical fiction." Right from the
first page MacDonald tells Ranald Bannerman's story through the

voice of Ranald himself—in the first person. This adds to the sense the reader has throughout that the events recorded here are real.

During this particular period of George MacDonald's life, when he was in his mid-forties and most of his eleven children were between five and nineteen years old, he did some of his finest writing for young people. I'm sure that's not by accident, for he was often thinking of his own sons and daughters, as well as his own boyhood, when telling stories on paper.

Therefore, we can conclude that many of the incidents in this book, *The Adventures of Ranald Bannerman*, are things that probably happened. Not everything, of course—but much of it—because this is, after all, a *story* MacDonald told. And realizing this makes Ranald all the more a personal friend. Because in a way, he's a picture of young George MacDonald.

Michael Phillips

SOME OPENING
THOUGHTS

I have always wanted to write the story of my own boyhood, and have determined now is the time.

However, I do not intend to carry it one month beyond the hour I saw that my boyhood was gone and my youth arrived. The reason for telling this first portion of my history is this: When I look back upon my boyhood, it seems to me not only so pleasant, but so full of meaning, that if I can just tell it right, it may also be pleasant and meaningful to those of you who will read it.

I suppose the story will prove very dull to those who care only for exciting adventures full of impossible things. But if you happen to be one of those who find your *own* life interesting, and simply *being* in the world is a pleasant thing, then I hope you will find the experience of a boy born in a very different position from you interesting.

That boy happens to be me. I am Ranald Bannerman, a Scotsman. My father was the clergyman of a country parish in the north of Scotland. His was a humble position, and our family lived plainly in every way. There was a little farm attached to the minister's house where we lived. My father rented some other land besides, for he needed to do as much farming as possible to add to the small amount he was paid by the church.

My mother was an invalid as far back as I can remember. We were four boys, and had no sister.

And now it is time for me to begin telling the story of my boyhood. To do so I must begin at the beginning, or at least as far back as it is possible.

Chapter Two

MY FIRST MEMORIES

I don't suppose any of you can tell when you first began to come awake to life, or what it was that wakened you. Neither can I.

I cannot recall when I began to remember, or what first got set down into my mind as worth remembering. Sometimes I think it must have been a tremendous flood that first made me wonder, and so made me begin to remember. Because it does seem to me that images of a flood are about as far distant in my beginnings of memory as anything.

When I close my eyes I can picture rain pouring so thick that I put my hand out in front of me to see whether I could see it through the blanket of falling water. There was a river that ran in the bottom of a little hollow a ways from our house. Usually you could see only little glimpses of it. It was hardly more than a little stream. But on this particular occasion the river was spread out like a sea in front of the house and stretched up and down in both directions farther than I could see.

Actually, the stream seemed to flood so often—every autumn in fact—that I have no confidence that one of these floods is in reality the oldest I remember.

Indeed, now that I think of it, I suspect my oldest memories are dreams. Where or when I dreamed them, only the God who made me knows.

Dreams quickly fade upon awakening, and therefore nearly all are very vague to me now. But they were almost all made up of bright things.

I can recall only one with any detail. I dreamed it often and that is why I can remember it after all these years.

It was of the room I slept in, only it was narrower in the dream, and higher, and the window was gone. But the ceiling was a ceiling indeed, for the sun, moon, and stars lived there.

The sun was not a scientific sun at all, but one such as you see in picture books—a round, jolly, smiling man's face, with flashes of yellow all around the edges of it, just like what a grand sunflower would look like if you set a face in where the black seeds are. And the moon was just such a one as you would see the cow jumping over in the pictured nursery rhyme. She was a crescent moon, of course, so that she might have a face drawn in the hollow, and turned toward the sun, who seemed to be her husband. He looked merrily at her, and she looked trustfully at him, and I knew that they got on very well together.

The stars were their children, of course, and they seemed to run about the ceiling just as they pleased. But the sun and the moon had regular motions. They rose and set at the proper times, for they were steady old folks.

I do not, however, remember ever seeing them rise or set. They were always up and near the center before the dream dawned on me.

It would always come to me in the same way. I thought I was waking up in the middle of the night, and there would be the room with the sun and the moon and the stars at their pranks and games in the ceiling!—Mr. Sun nodding and smiling across the space to Mrs. Moon, and she nodding back to him with a knowing look, and the corners of her mouth drawn down.

I have vague memories of having heard them talk. At times I feel as if I could yet recall something of what they said, but it vanishes the moment I try to catch it. It was very peculiar talk indeed—about me, I thought—but it seemed to make sense during the dream.

When the dream had been particularly vivid, I would sometimes think of it in the middle of the next day, and look up to the sun, saying to myself, "He's up there now, busy enough. I wonder what he is seeing to talk to his wife about when he comes down at night." I think it sometimes made me a little more careful of my conduct. When the sun set in the evening, I thought he was going into the house the back way. And when the moon rose, I thought she was going out for a little stroll until I should go to sleep, when they would both come into my room and talk about me again.

Although I never fancied it of the sun, I thought I could make the moon follow me as I pleased. I remember once my eldest brother making me very angry by bursting into laughter when I offered, in all seriousness, to bring her to the other side of the house where they wanted light to go on with something they were about in the darkness.

But I must return to my dream, for I have not yet told you the most remarkable thing about it. In one corner of the ceiling there was a hole, and through that hole came down a ladder of sunrays—very bright and lovely. Where it came from I never thought about. But of course it could not have come from the sun, because there he was, with his bright coat off, playing the father of his family in the most homely Old-English-gentleman fashion possible.

But that it was a ladder of rays there could be no doubt. *If only I could climb upon it*, I thought! I often tried, but as fast as I lifted my feet to climb, down they came again upon the boards of the floor of my room. At length I did succeed, but this time the dream had a real setting.

I have said that we were four boys; however, at this time we were five—there was a little baby. He was very ill, and I knew he was not expected to live. I remember looking out of my bed one night and seeing my mother bending over him in her lap—it is one of the few things I do remember about my mother. I fell asleep, and by and by awoke and looked out again.

No one was there. Not only were mother and baby gone, but the cradle was gone too. I knew that my little brother was dead. I did not cry. I was too young and ignorant to cry about it. I went to sleep again, and seemed to wake once more, but it was into my dream this time.

There were the sun and the moon and the stars. But the sun and the moon had got close together and were talking very ear-

nestly, with all the stars gathered round them. I could not hear a word they said, but I concluded they were talking about my little brother.

In the meantime I observed a curious motion in the heavenly host. They kept looking at me and then at the corner where the ladder stood, and talking away, for I saw their lips moving very fast, and I thought by the motion of them that they were saying something about the ladder.

I got out of my bed and went to it. If I could only climb up it! I tried once more. To my delight I found that it would hold me. I climbed and climbed, and the sun and the moon and the stars looked more and more pleased as I got up nearer to them till at last the sun's face was in a broad smile. But they did not move from their places, and my head rose above them, and got out at the hole where the ladder came in at the ceiling.

What I saw there above the roof of our house, I cannot tell. I only know that a wind blew upon me such as had never blown upon me in my waking hours. I did not care much for kisses then, for I had not learned how good they are. But somehow I fancied afterward that the wind was made of my baby brother's kisses. And I began to love the little man who had lived only long enough to be our brother and get up above the sun and the stars by the ladder of the sunrays.

But all this I thought afterward. All I can remember of my dream is that I began to weep for very delight of something I had forgotten, and that I fell down the ladder into the room again and awoke as one always does with a fall in a dream. Sun, moon, and stars were gone. The ladder of light had vanished, and I lay sobbing on my pillow.

MY MOTHER

I have taken a good deal of time with this story of a dream, but it remained with me and would often return. And then the time of life when it came to me, so also like a dream itself that telling of the sun and moon in my room seems to fit right in. There is a twilight of the mind when all things are strange, and when the memory is only beginning to know that it has a notebook and must put things down in it.

It was not long after this that my mother died. I was sorrier for my father than for myself—he looked so sad.

I have said that as far back as I can remember, she was an invalid. Hence she was unable to be with us much. She is very beautiful in my memory, but during the last months of her life we seldom saw her, and the desire to keep the house quiet for her sake must have been the beginning of that freedom which we enjoyed during the whole of our boyhood. So we were out every day and all day long, finding our meals when we pleased, and often without even going home for them.

I remember her death clearly, but will not dwell upon that. It is too sad to write much about, though she was happy and the least troubled of us all. Her only concern was at having to leave husband and children. But the will of God was a better thing to her than to live with her family. My sorrow at least was soon over. For God makes children so that grief cannot cling to them. They must not begin life with a burden of loss. He knows it is only for a time. When I see my mother again, she will not be upset that my tears were so soon dried.

"Little one," I think I hear her saying, "how could you go on crying for your poor mother when God was mothering you all the time, breathing life into you, and making the world a blessed place for you? You will tell me all about it someday."

Yes, and we shall tell our mothers, shall we not, how sorry we are that we ever gave them any trouble. Sometimes we were very naughty, and sometimes we did not know better.

My mother was very good, but I cannot remember a single one of the many kisses she must have given me. I remember her holding my head to her bosom when she was dying—that is all.

CHAPTER
FOUR
—

MY FATHER

My father was a tall, serious, solemn man, who walked slowly with long strides. He spoke very little, and generally looked as if he were pondering next Sunday's sermon. His head was gray and a little bent, as if he were gathering truth from the ground.

Once I came upon him in the garden, standing with his face up to heaven, and I thought he was seeing something in the clouds. But when I came nearer I saw that his eyes were closed and it made me feel very solemn. I crept away as if I had been looking where I shouldn't have.

He did not talk much to us. What he said was very gentle, and it seemed to me it was his seriousness that made him gentle. I have seen him look very angry. He used to walk much about his fields, especially on summer mornings before the sun was up. This was after my mother's death. I think he felt nearer to her in the fields than in the house.

There was a kind of grandeur about him, I am sure. For I never saw one of his parishioners greet him on the road without a look of my father himself passing like a solemn cloud over the face of the man or woman. For us, we both feared and loved him at once.

I do not remember ever being punished by him, but Kirsty (of whom I shall tell you about after a while) has told me that he did punish us when we were very small children. Neither did he teach us much about himself, except on the few times I am about to mention. And I cannot say that I learned much from his sermons.

His preaching seemed to please those of his parishioners whom I heard speak of it, because they always seemed to be saying nice things about my father's sermons. But although I loved the sound of his voice, and liked to look at his face as he stood up there in the ancient pulpit in his gown, I never cared much about what he said. Of course it was a better sermon than any other minister could have preached, though what it was all about mattered nothing to me.

In the same way that I assumed his sermons to be the best, I likewise never had the least doubt that my father was the best man in the world. And to this very hour I am of the same opinion, despite the fact that the son of the village tailor once gave me a tremendous thrashing for saying so. He said I was altogether wrong, seeing that *his* father was the best man in the world! From the experience, I have at least learned to modify my assertion only to this extent—that my father was the best man I have ever known.

The church was a very old one—so old, in fact, that it seemed to be settling down again into the earth, especially on one side, where great buttresses had been built to keep it from falling. It leaned against them like a weary old thing that wanted to go to sleep. It had a short square tower like so many of the churches in England. There was only an old cracked bell, and no organ, or chanting worshipers or singing choir. But even without any of these things, the awe and reverence which fell upon me as I crossed its worn threshold were as great as anyone else might feel when entering the most beautiful churches of the south. There was a hush in it, which seemed to demand a soft footstep as if one were walking on holy ground. And the church was inseparably associated with my father.

The pew we sat in was square, with a table in the middle of it for our books. My brother David generally used it for laying his head on, so that he might go to sleep comfortably. My brother Tom put his feet on its crossbar, leaned back in his corner—for you see we had a corner apiece—put his hands in his pants' pockets, and stared hard at my father. My brother Allister, whose back was to the pulpit, used to look at a book during the sermon. But I was happiest of all. For in my position I could look up at my father if I pleased, a little sideways. Or, if I preferred, I could gaze at the figure of an armed knight, carved in stone, which lay at the top of the tomb in front of the church of Sir Worm Wymble. At least that is the nearest I can come to the spelling of the name they gave him.

Tombs of famous personalities are common enough in the churches of England, but are a rare sight in Scotch churches. This particular tomb stood in a hollow in the wall, and the knight lay under the arch of the recess, so silent, so patient, with folded palms, as if praying for some help which he could not name. The presence of the dead knight with the carved stone above him, lying there with face upturned as if looking to heaven, gave a certain feel to the place that it wouldn't have possessed otherwise.

But from gazing at the knight, I began to regard the wall about him and the arch over him. And from the arch my eye would go up to the roof, and then about to the various pillars, then wander about the windows, and so all over the whole inside of the building, looking at the various points of strength and wondering how it managed to hold itself up. So while my father was talking about the church as a company of believers and describing how it was held together by faith, I was trying to understand how the stone and cement of the old place kept from falling down. And thus it was that I began to follow what has become my profession now that I am grown, for I am an architect.

But talking about the church itself has led me away from my father, and I want to finish telling you about him. He always spoke in a rather low voice, but so earnestly that every eye was fixed upon him. Every eye, that is, except mine and those of two of my brothers. And even Tom, with all his staring, knew as little about the sermon as any of us. But my father did not seem to mind, and never questioned us about anything he had said. He did what was far better.

On Sunday afternoons, in the warm, peaceful sunlight of summer, with the honeysuckle filling the air of the little garden where we sat, he would sit for an hour talking away to us in his gentle, slow, deep voice, telling us story after story out of the New Testament, and explaining them in a way I have seldom heard equalled.

Or on cold winter nights, he would come into the room where I and my two younger brothers slept. He would then sit down with Tom by his side in front of a fire that burned bright in the frosty air, would open the great family Bible on the table, turn his face toward the two beds where we three lay wide awake, and tell us story after story out of the Old Testament. Sometimes he would read a few verses, turning the bare faces into an expanded and illustrated story of his own which he would set in our own country and time.

We lay and listened with all the more enjoyment, knowing that while the fire was burning so brightly and the presence of my father was filling the room with safety and peace, the wind was howling outside, and the snow was drifting up against the window. Sometimes I passed into the land of sleep with his voice in my ears and his love in my heart—perhaps into the land of visions, and once into a dream of the sun and moon and stars bowing down to the favored son of Jacob.

CHAPTER FIVE

—

KIRSTY

My father had a housekeeper whom he considered a very trusty woman. We thought her *very* old. I suppose she was about forty.

She was not pleasant, for she was grim-faced and critical, with a very straight back and a long upper lip. Indeed, the distance from her nose to her mouth was greater than the length of her nose.

When she first comes to my mind it is always as making some complaint to my father against us boys. Perhaps she meant to speak the truth. Or rather perhaps she took it for granted that she always did speak the truth. But she would always exaggerate things and make them look quite different from the way they really happened. The bones of her story might be true, but she would put a skin over it of her own design, which was not loving or nice toward us and made us always look as if we had been doing wrong.

The result was that the older we grew, the more our minds were separated from her, and the more we came to regard her as our enemy. If she really meant to be our friend in the best way she knew, it was certainly an unfriendly kind of friendship. For whatever it was, it displayed itself in constant opposition, fault-finding, criticism, accusation, and complaint.

The real mistake was simply that we were boys. There was

something in her that just altogether did not like the boy nature. You would have thought that to be a boy was in her eyes something very wrong to begin with, that boys ought never to have been made, that they must always, by their very nature, be about something underhanded and devious. I have occasionally wondered how she would have behaved to a girl. On thinking about it, I think a little better, but the girl would have been worse off because she could not have escaped from her as we did. My father would hear her complaints to the end without saying a single word, unless it was to ask a question. When she had finished, he would turn again to his book or sermon, saying, "Very well, Mrs. Mitchell, I will speak to them about it."

My impression is that he did not believe half of what she told him. In any event, when he had sent for us, he would ask us our version of the affair, and listen to us just as he had listened to her. Then he would set forth to us where we had been wrong, if we were wrong, and send us away with a reminder not to bother Mrs. Mitchell, who couldn't help being a little short tempered, poor thing! Somehow or other we got it into our heads that the shortness of her temper was mysteriously associated with the shortness of her nose.

She was frugal, to the point of outright stinginess. She would do her best to provide what my father liked, but for us she thought almost anything good enough. She would give us the thinnest of the milk—we said that she thinned the cream out of it three times before she thought it watery enough to give to us. My two younger brothers did not mind it so much as I did, for I was always rather delicate, and if I didn't like something I would rather go without than to eat or drink it.

In any case, I have told you enough to make it plain that she was not a favorite with us.

Now, for the description of Kirsty, the other woman about the place, who *was* our favorite—our good and kind ally whom we would go to whenever we had troubles of any kind.

Kirsty was a Highland woman who had charge of the house in which the farm servants lived, which sat about two hundred yards away from our own house. She was a cheerful, gracious, and kind woman—the kind of person about whom one would say she was a woman of God's making. Though that brings up the mysterious truth that cannot be denied; God must have made Mrs. Mitchell too. I still find the whole thing very puzzling.

I remember once when my youngest brother Davie, a very little fellow then, for he could not speak plainly, came running to Kirsty in great distress, crying, "Fee, fee!" by which he meant that a flea was making his life miserable. Kirsty at once undressed him and began the hunt. After a successful search, while she was putting on his clothes again, little Davie became very solemn and thoughtful.

"God didn't make the fees, Kirsty!" he said.

"Oh yes, Davie! God made everything. God did make the fleas."

Davie was silent for a while. Then he opened his mouth and spoke like an annoyed prophet of the Old Testament.

"Then why doesn't he give them something else to eat?"

"You must ask him that yourself," said Kirsty, with a wisdom I have since learned to understand.

The whole conversation set me to thinking too. Before Davie was fully dressed, I had *my* question to put to Kirsty. Actually it was the same question, only with a more important object in the eye of it.

"Then I suppose God must have made Mrs. Mitchell as well as you and the rest of us, Kirsty?" I questioned.

"Certainly, Ranald," returned Kirsty.

"Well, I wish he hadn't," was my remark.

"Oh, she's not a bad sort," said Kirsty; "though I must say if I were she, I would try to be a little more agreeable."

Despite the distance to the farmhouse, even if one of us had a cut finger with blood pouring out of it, our feet would run the whole way without hesitation rather than go to Mrs. Mitchell for help.

Kirsty was short and slender, with keen blue eyes and dark hair, a light step, a sweet voice, and a generous hand. But of course there I am describing her moral nature, for it is the mind that makes the hand generous. I can hardly tell a thing about her face because it was so entirely the sign of good to me and my brothers. I loved her so much that I do not know now, just as I did not care when I was a boy, whether she was nice-looking or not. I'm sure she was just as old as Mrs. Mitchell, but we never thought of *her* being old. She was our refuge in all times of trouble and necessity. She gave us something to eat as often and as much as we wanted. She used to say it was no cheating of the minister to feed the minister's boys. And then her stories! There was nothing like them in all the countryside! Actually, it was a rather dreary country to gaze on. It had many bleak moorland hills that were not high but very desolate. But Kirsty herself had come from a region of the Highlands where the hills were hills indeed—hills with mighty skeletons of stone inside them, hills that looked as if they had been heaped over huge monsters which were now always trying to get up. It was a country where every cliff and rock had its own story—and Kirsty's head was full of them! It was a delight indeed to sit by her fire and listen to them after the men had had their supper and gone home.

Sitting by Kirsty's fire, listening to her stories, we were in our heaven!

—

I BEGIN LIFE

I began the life of what might be called my childhood, as near as I can guess, about the age of six. It was not a pleasant experience.

One glorious morning in early summer I found myself led by the ungentle hand of Mrs. Mitchell toward a little school on the outside of the village. It was run by an old woman called Mrs. Shand, and the school was in her home. In an English village I think she would have been called Dame Shand. We, being Scottish, called her Luckie Shand.

As I was half-dragged along the road by Mrs. Mitchell, I kept attempting in vain to pull my hand out of her rough grasp. I looked around at the shining fields and up at the blue sky, where I saw a lark singing as if he had just found out that he could sing. But in my heart was the despair of a man on his way to be hanged at the gallows, and I had the feeling that I was bidding farewell to the world.

We had to cross a little stream, and when we reached the middle of the footbridge, I tugged again at my imprisoned hand. I think somewhere in my head was the half-formed idea of throwing myself over the edge and into the brook. But my efforts accomplished nothing. The big hand had mine in a vice and would not let it go!

Mrs. Mitchell continued pulling me along the road for a half mile or so, and I was getting wearier every step from sheer un-willingness. At length I was led to the cottage door. It was no cottage like you will probably picture in your mind—with roses and honeysuckle covering its walls, and hedges and plants around, and thatch on the roof, everything looking altogether pleasant and homey. No, it was a dreary little house of brown stone with nothing green on the walls or growing anywhere about it. In front was an open ditch, with a stone slab over it for a bridge.

Did I say there was nothing on the walls? That is not altogether right. On this morning there was the loveliest sunshine. And that made it all the worse, for even the brightness of the day I was going to leave behind when I went in behind those dreary, cold brown stones. The whole thing was especially bitter since I had expected to spend the day with my elder brother at a neighboring farm, and now suddenly here I was in front of the prison!

Mrs. Mitchell opened the door and led me in. It was an awful experience. Luckie Shand stood at her table ironing. She was as tall as Mrs. Mitchell, and that was enough to prejudice me against her immediately. She wore a close-fitting widow's cap, with a black ribbon round it. Her hair was gray, and her face was as gray as her hair, and her skin was gathered in wrinkles about her mouth, where they twitched and twitched, as if she were constantly thinking something unpleasant. She looked up.

"I've brought you a new scholar," said Mrs. Mitchell.

"Well . . . very well," replied the dame in a dubious tone. "I hope he's a good boy, for he must be good if he comes here."

"Well, he's just middling. His father spares the rod, Mrs. Shand, and we know what comes of that."

They went on with their talk, which, as far as I can recall, was complimentary to none but the two women themselves. In the meantime I was looking about and making what observations I could in the midst of my terror. About a dozen children were seated on long benches along the walls, peering over the tops of their spelling books at the newcomer. In the far corner two were kicking at each other as they had the opportunity, looking very angry but not daring to make a sound or cry out.

My next discovery was a terrible one. Some movement drew my eyes to the floor. There I saw a boy of my own age on his hands

27

and knees, fastened by a string to a leg of the table at which the dame was ironing. And as horrible as it is to tell, a dog lay under the table watching him. It was not a very big dog, but ugly, and certainly big enough to be frightened at. I gazed at the boy and dog in dismay.

"Ah, you may look!" said the dame. "If you're not a good boy, that is what shall happen to you. The dog will have to make you mind."

I trembled and said nothing. After some further discussion Mrs. Mitchell left, saying, "I'll come back for him at one o'clock, and if I don't, just keep him till I do come."

The dame accompanied her back to the door, and then I discovered that she was lame and hobbled quite badly. An instant resolution formed in my brain.

I sat down on the bench near the door and kept very quiet. Had it not been for what I was thinking, I am sure I should have cried. When the dame returned, she resumed her ironing. Then after a moment she called me to her by name. I obeyed, trembling.

"Can you say your letters?" she asked.

Now although I could not read, I could repeat the alphabet. How I had learned it, I do not know. I repeated it then for her.

"How many questions of your catechism can you say?" she asked next. Not knowing for sure what she meant, I said nothing.

"No sulking!" said the dame. Opening a drawer in the table, she took out the book of the catechism and handed it to me.

"Go to your seat," she said. I obeyed, and with the book before me pondered my plan.

Everything depended on whether I could open the door before she could reach me. Once out of the house I was sure of running faster than she could follow.

The ironing, of course, required a fire to make the irons hot. And as the morning went on, the sunshine on the walls, working with the fire on the hearth, made the place too hot for the comfort of the old dame. She went and opened the door wide. I was instantly on the alert, watching for an opportunity.

One soon occurred.

A class of some five or six was reading out of the Bible, if reading it could be called. At length it came to the turn of one who blundered dreadfully. It was the same boy who had been tied under the table, but he had been released for his lesson. The dame hobbled to him and found he had his book upside down. She turned angrily back to the table, opened the drawer again, and this time took from it a long leather strap. With it she proceeded to whip him. As his first cry reached my ears I was halfway to the door. On the threshold I stumbled and fell.

"The new boy's running away!" shrieked some little traitor inside.

I heard the words with horror, but was up and off in a moment. But I had not got many yards from the cottage before I heard the voice of the dame screaming after me to return. I took no heed, and ran all the faster.

Then after a moment my horror increased. For suddenly I was aware that her commands were being enforced by the pursuing bark of her prime minister. I was paralyzed with fear. I turned to glance behind me, and there was the fiendish-looking dog close on my heels. I could run no longer. For one moment I felt as if I should sink to the earth in sheer terror.

But then the next instant a great rage sent the blood to my brain. From cowardice I was suddenly filled with wild attack—I cannot call it courage. I spun around and rushed toward the little wretch. I had no idea how to fight him, but in desperation I threw myself upon him and dug my fingernails into him. Fortunately they found their way into his eyes.

He turned out to be a great coward of a dog. He yelped and howled and struggled from my grasp. Then he turned with his tail bent low and ran back to his mistress, who was hobbling after me. But with the renewed strength of triumph I turned again for home, and ran as I had never run before. When or where the dame gave up the chase, I do not know. I never turned my head around again until I laid it on Kirsty's bosom, and there I burst out sobbing and crying. It was the only sound I had left in me.

As soon as Kirsty had succeeded in calming me, I told her the whole story. She said little, but I could see she was very angry. No doubt she was pondering what she ought to do. She got me some milk—actually it was half cream I do believe, and tasted so good— and some oatcake, and went on with her work.

While I ate I reflected that any moment Mrs. Mitchell might appear to drag me back in disgrace to that horrible den. I knew that Kirsty's authority was not as great as hers, and that she would have no choice but to give me up. Therefore, I watched for an opportunity to escape once more and hide myself so Kirsty might be able to say she did not know where I was.

When I had finished my oatcake and cream, and Kirsty had left the kitchen for a moment, I sped quietly to the door and looked out into the farmyard. There was no one to be seen. The dark, brown, cool door of the barn stood open as if inviting me to shelter and safety, for I knew that in the darkest end of it lay a great heap of oat straw.

I ran across the space of sunshine into the darkness, across the cool floor, and immediately began burrowing in the straw like a wild animal. I drew out handfuls and laid them carefully aside so that the pile wouldn't look disorderly and betray my presence. When I had made a hole large enough to hold me, I got in. I then kept drawing out the straw behind me, and filling in the hole in front. I continued this until I not only had stopped up the entrance, but also had placed a good thickness of straw between me and the outside.

By the time I had burrowed as far as I thought necessary, I was quite tired. I lay down at full length in my hole, delighting in a sense of safety such as I had never before experienced. I was soon fast asleep.

Chapter Seven

THE HEART OF REFUGE

I awoke, crept out of my lair, and peeped out the door of the barn. The sun was already going down.

I discovered that I was getting hungry. I went out the door at the other end into the farmyard and ran across to the farmhouse. No one was there. Something moved me to climb up on the bench and look out of a little window, from which I could see our house and the road from it. To my dismay, there was Mrs. Mitchell coming toward the farm!

I possessed my wits enough to run first to Kirsty's cupboard and grab a good supply of oatcakes. With them in my hand I sped like a hunted rabbit to its burrow, out the back door and back to the barn. I had soon drawn out the straw I had plugged into the mouth of the hole, and again crept inside. Hearing no one approach, I began to eat the oatcakes and fell fast asleep again before I had finished them.

As I slept I dreamed my dream. The sun was looking very serious, and the moon reflected his concern. They were not satisfied with me.

At length the sun shook his head—that is, his whole self rotated back and forth—and the moon shook herself in response. Then they nodded to each other as if to say, "That is entirely my own opinion." At last they began to talk, not as men do, but both speaking at once, yet each listening while each spoke. I heard no word, but their lips moved most busily. Their eyebrows went up and down, their eyelids winked and winked, and their cheeks puckered and relaxed incessantly. There was an absolute storm of expression on their faces, and their noses twisted and curled.

As for the stars, they darted all about, gathered into groups, shot about again, then formed into new groups. They had no faces. But being sort of celestial tadpoles, they indicated by their motions alone that they took an active interest in the questions of such concern to their parents.

Finally I could bear it no longer, and awoke.

I was in darkness, though not in my own bed. When I proceeded to turn, I found myself stuck and scratched on all sides. I could not stretch my arms, and there was hardly any room for my body. At first I was dreadfully frightened. But as my brain awoke, I recalled the horrible school, the horrible schoolmistress, and the most horrible dog. But with thought of the dog came a rejoicing, with the pride of a dragon slayer, in my victory.

Next, I thought it would be good to look about again and see what was up. I drew away the straw from the entrance to my cave; but to my dismay I found that when my hand went out into space, no light came through the opening.

What could it mean? Surely I had not grown blind while I lay asleep! Hurriedly I shot out of the hole. In the huge barn there was but the dullest glimmer of light. I tumbled my way toward one of the doors. I found it bolted, but this one I knew was fastened on the inside with a wooden bolt which I could draw back.

The open door revealed the dark night. Before me was the grain yard full of the ricks of stacked grain. Tall and dim they rose between me and the sky. I turned and looked back into the barn. It appeared a horrible cave filled with darkness. Suddenly I remembered there were rats in it! I dared not enter it again, even to go out at the opposite door. I completely forgot how soundly and peacefully I had slept in it.

I stepped out into the night, with the shadowy ricks about me and the awful vault of heaven over my head. I half groped my way through the stands and got out into the open field. I had never before known what night was. The real sting of its fear lay in this—that there was nobody else in it. There I stood in the vast hall of the silent night—alone. Everybody besides me was asleep all over the world, and had abandoned me to my fate, whatever might come out of the darkness to seize me.

When I got round the edge of a stone wall I saw the moon—crescent, as I saw her in my dream, but low down toward the horizon and lying almost upon her rounded back. She looked very sad and dim. Even she would take no heed of me! The stars were high up, away in the heavens. They did not look like the children of the sun and moon at all, and *they* took no heed of me. Yet at the same time there was a grandeur in my desolation that would have lifted my heart if it had not been for the fear.

A stupid calf gave out a dull sleepy low and startled me dreadfully. If I but had one living creature at my side as I stood staring about me! Even the calf would do! But still I was alone.

It was not dark out here in the open field, for at this season of the year it is not dark there all night long. Toward the north I gazed at the pale light of the sunken sun who was even now creeping round toward the spot in the east where he would rise again.

And all at once I remembered that God was near me. But then I did not know who God is as I know now. And when I thought about him then, which was neither much nor often, my idea of him was not really like him. It was merely a confused mixture of other people's fancies, as well as my own, about him. I had not learned how beautiful God is. I had only learned that he is strong. I had been told that he was angry with those who did wrong. I had not understood that he loved them all the time, although he was displeased with them and must punish them to make them good. When I thought of him now in the silent starry night, a yet greater terror seized me, and I ran stumbling over the uneven field.

Where should I fly but home? True, Mrs. Mitchell was there. But there was another there as well. Even Kirsty would not do in this terror. Home was the only refuge, for my father was there. I sped for the manse.

But as I approached our house a new fear laid hold of my trembling heart. I was not sure, but I thought the door was always locked at night. I drew nearer. The place of refuge rose before me.

I stood on the little plot of grass in front of it. There was no light in its eyes. Its mouth was closed. It was silent as one of the ricks of grain. Above it were the speechless stars. Nothing was alive. Nothing would speak.

I went up the few rough granite steps that led to the door. I laid my hand on the handle and gently turned it. Joy of joys, the door opened!

I entered the hall. It was even more silent than the night. No footsteps echoed. No voices were there.

I closed the door behind me, and, almost sick with the misery of being where no other human being was, I groped my way to my father's room. When I had my hand on his door, the warm tide of courage began again to flow from my heart. I opened the door very quietly, for was not the dragon asleep down below?

"Papa! Papa!" I cried in an eager whisper. "Are you awake, Papa?" No voice came in reply. The place was yet more silent than the night or the hall. He must be asleep. I was afraid to call louder. I crept nearer to his bed. I stretched out my hands to feel for him. He must be at the farther side. I climbed up on the bed. I felt all across it. Utter desertion seized my soul—my father was not there! Was it a horrible dream? I fell down on the bed weeping bitterly, and wept myself asleep.

How much time passed I do not know. Once more I awoke to a sense of misery. I stretched out my arms and cried, "Papa! Papa!" The same moment I found my father's arms around me. He folded me close to him.

"Hush, Ranald, my boy!" he said. "Here I am. You are quite safe."

"Oh, Papa!" I sobbed, "I thought I had lost you."

"And I thought I had lost you, my boy. Tell me all about it."

Between my narrative and my replies to his questions he soon had the whole story. And then I learned the dismay of the household when I did not appear. Kirsty told what she knew. They searched everywhere, but could not find me. As great as had been my misery, my father's had been greater. While I stood forsaken and desolate in the field, they had been searching for my drowned body along the banks of the river.

The young cowherd who slept at the farmhouse ran back from

the river to the farm. They had already searched it and every place they could think of. But now he had a new thought and decided to look again about the barn. Eventually he came to the pile of straw, saw the scattered bits of it about, and thus guided found my deserted lair. He ran back to the riverside with the news. When my father returned, he failed to find me in my own bed, but then to his infinite relief found me fast asleep on his. He undressed me and laid me in the bed without my once opening my eyes—strange as I had already slept so long. But sorrow is very sleepy.

Having in this way felt the awfulness and majesty of the heavens at night, it was a very long time before I dreamed again my childish dreams.

CHAPTER
EIGHT

MRS. MITCHELL
IS DEFEATED

After this talk with my father, I fell into a sleep of perfect contentment. I never thought a thing of what might come in the morning.

But the instant I awoke I grew aware of the danger I was in of being carried off once more to school. Indeed, unless my father interfered, the thing was almost inevitable. I thought he would protect me, but I could not be sure. He was gone when I woke up, for as I have mentioned already, he was given to going out early in the mornings. It was not that early now, however, for I had slept much longer than usual. I got up at once, intending to find him. But to my horror, before I was half dressed, my enemy Mrs. Mitchell came into the room looking triumphant and revengeful.

"I'm glad to see you're getting up," she said. "It's nearly schooltime." The tone of her voice and the way she pronounced the word *school* would have been enough to reveal what she was thinking of me, even if her eyes had not been fierce with smoldering anger.

"I haven't had my porridge," I said.

"Your porridge is waiting for you—as cold as stone," she answered. "If boys will lie in bed so late, what can they expect?"

"Nothing from you," I muttered.

"What's that you're saying?" she asked angrily. I was silent. "Hurry up," she went on. "I don't want you to keep me waiting all day."

"You don't have to wait, Mrs. Mitchell. I am dressing as fast as I can. Is Papa in his study yet?"

"No, and you needn't think to see him. I'm sure he's angry enough with you already."

She little knew what had passed between my father and me already. She could not imagine what a talk we had.

"And don't think you'll be able to run away as you did yesterday. I know all about it. Mrs. Shand told me everything. I shouldn't wonder if your papa's gone to see her now, and tell her how sorry he is you were so naughty."

"I'm not going to school."

"We'll see about that."

"I tell you I won't go."

"And I tell you we'll see about it."

"I won't go till I've seen Papa. If he says I'm to go, I will go. But I won't go for you."

"You *will* go, and you *won't* see him!" she repeated, standing staring at me, as I slowly, but with hands trembling partly from fear, partly from anger, continued to fasten up my clothes.

"Now wash your face," she added.

"I won't so long as you're standing there," I said, and sat down on the floor. She began to walk toward me.

"If you touch me I'll scream!" I cried.

She stopped, thought for a moment, then turned and left the room. But I heard her turn the key outside and lock the door.

I proceeded to finish my dressing as fast as I could. The moment I was ready, I opened the window, which was only a few feet from the ground, scrambled through the opening, and dropped. I hurt myself a little, but not too much, and fled for the harbor of Kirsty's arms. But as I turned the corner of the house I ran straight into Mrs. Mitchell, who received me with not a very soft embrace. In fact, I was rather severely scratched with a pin in her dress.

"It serves you right," she said when I cried out. "That's a judgment on you for trying to run away again. After all the trouble you gave us yesterday too! You are a bad boy."

"Why am I a bad boy?"

"It's bad not to do what you are told."

"I will do what my papa tells me."

"Your papa! There are more people in the world than your papa."

"So I'm a bad boy if I don't do what anybody like you chooses to tell me?"

"None of your impudence!"

Her statement was accompanied by a box on the ear. She was now dragging me into the kitchen. There she set my porridge before me, which I did not eat.

"Well, if you won't eat good food, you shall go to school without it."

"I tell you I won't go to school."

She grabbed me up in her arms. She was very strong, and there was nothing I could do to prevent her from carrying me out of the house. If I had been the bad boy she said I was, I could have bitten and scratched and soon forced her to set me down. But I felt I must not do that, for then I would be ashamed before my father. So I yielded to my fate for the time, and fell to planning.

I was not long in coming to a resolution. I managed to draw out the long pin that had scratched me from her dress. I did not believe she would carry me very far, but if she did not set me down soon I resolved to make her. I resolved further that when we came to the footbridge, which had but one rail to it, if she was still carrying me, I would run the pin into her and make her let me go. When she did I would instantly throw myself into the river. I would run the risk of being drowned rather than go to that school.

My whole blood was boiling. I was convinced that my father could not be party to all this, and that *he* hadn't directed that I be treated in such a manner. He could not have been so kind and gentle and understanding in the night, and then send me to such a place in the morning.

But happily things did not become so desperate as in my imaginings. Before we were out of the gate, my heart leaped for joy. For I heard my father calling, "Mrs. Mitchell! Mrs. Mitchell!"

I looked around. I saw him coming after us with his long slow strides, and I fell to struggling so violently that she was glad enough to set me down. I broke free and ran to my father and burst out crying.

"Papa! Papa!" I sobbed, "don't send me to that horrid school. I can learn to read without that old woman to teach me."

"Really, Mrs. Mitchell," said my father, taking me by the hand and leading me toward her. "Really, Mrs. Mitchell, you are taking too much upon yourself! The education of my sons is hardly something I approve of your taking into your own hands in this way. I never said the child was to go to that woman's school."

Mrs. Mitchell stood still, visibly flaming with rage and annoyance. "In fact, I don't approve of what I hear of her," my father went on, "and I have thought of consulting with some of my brethren in the presbytery on the matter before taking steps myself. I won't have the young people in my parish oppressed in such a fashion. And using dogs to strike terror too! It is shameful."

"She's a very decent woman, Mistress Shand," said the housekeeper.

"I don't doubt her decency, Mrs. Mitchell. But I doubt very much whether she is fit to have charge of children. Since she is a friend of yours, you will be doing her a kindness to give her a hint to that effect. It may save me from being forced to take further and more unpleasant steps against her."

"Indeed, sir, it would be a hard thing to take the bread out of the mouth of one lone widow woman, and bring her upon the parish with a bad name besides. She's supported herself for years with her school, and been a trouble to nobody."

"Except the lambs of the flock, Mrs. Mitchell. I commend you for standing up for your friend. But is a woman, because she is alone and a widow, to be allowed to exercise such cruelty? She may have been a teacher of some credibility once, but the reports are growing about her, and the day will come when I shall have to heed them. Perhaps I have already delayed too long. What I hear of her methods is enough to make idiots of some of the children. She had better see to a change, and soon. You tell her that—from me, if you like. And don't you meddle with school affairs. I'll take my young men," he added with a smile, "to school when I see fit."

"I asked your opinion, sir, before I took him," said Mrs. Mitchell.

"I believe I did say something about its being time he were able to read. But I recollect nothing more. You must have misunderstood me," he added, willing to ease her humiliation after his rebuke.

She walked away without another word, sniffing the air as she went, and carrying her hands folded under her apron. From that hour ever afterward, I believe she hated me.

My father watched her go with a smile, and then looked down on me and said, "She's short in temper, poor woman. We mustn't provoke her."

I was too well satisfied to urge my victory further by complaint. I could afford to let the matter drop, for I had been delivered from the fiery furnace, and suddenly the earth and sky were laughing around me. Oh, what sunshine filled the world! How glad were the larks, which are the praisers among the birds, that blessed morning!

CHAPTER
NINE
—
A NEW
SCHOOLMISTRESS

But, Ranald," my father continued as we slowly walked back toward the house, "what are we to do about the reading? I fear I may have let you go too long already."

"I don't know, Papa," I answered. "I can repeat the letters."

"I didn't want to make learning a burden to you," he went on, as if he hadn't heard me. "And I don't approve of children learning to read too soon. But at your age it is time you were beginning."

"You could teach me, Papa," I suggested hopefully.

"I have time to teach you some things, but I can't teach you everything. I have got to read a great deal and think a great deal, and go about my parish a good deal. And your brother Tom has heavy lessons to learn at school, and I have to help him. So what's to be done, Ranald, my boy? You can't go to the parish school with Tom before you can read."

"There's Kirsty, Papa," I suggested further.

"Yes, there's Kirsty," he returned with a sly smile. "Kirsty can do everything, can't she?"

"She can speak Gaelic," I said with a tone of triumph, mentioning her greatest accomplishment in my eyes.

"I wish you could speak Gaelic," said my father, thinking, I believe, of his wife, my mother, for whom it was the native tongue. "But that is not what is most important for you to learn. Do you think Kirsty could teach you to read English?"

"Yes, I do."

My father fell to thinking. "Let's go and ask her," he said, taking my hand.

I skipped along with positive delight. I did not stop my gleeful bounding about until we were standing on Kirsty's hard-packed dirt floor. She pulled out one of her pine chairs and dusted it off for the minister to sit on. She never called him *the master* but always *the minister*. She was a great favorite with my father, and he always behaved as a guest while at the farmhouse.

"Well, Kirsty," he said after the first greetings were over, "what would you think of turning yourself into a schoolmistress?"

"I would make a poor hand at that," she answered with a smile to me, which showed she guessed well enough what my father wanted. "But if I were to teach Master Ranald there, I would dearly like to try to see what I could do."

She always used *master* with our names, with the utmost of politeness. Mrs. Mitchell never did. The matter was soon settled between them.

"And if you want to beat him, Kirsty, you can do so in Gaelic, and then he won't feel it," said my father, attempting a joke, a not-so-common thing with him. Kirsty and I both laughed heartily.

The fact was, Kirsty had come to the manse with my mother, and my father was attached to her for the sake of his wife as well as for her own, and Kirsty would have died for the minister or any one of his boys. All the devotion a Highland woman has for the chief of her clan, Kirsty had for my father, not to mention the reverence due to the minister.

After a little chat about the cows and the calves, my father rose. "Then I'll just turn him over to you, Kirsty. Do you think you can manage without it interfering with your work?"

"Oh yes, sir! Easily enough. I shall soon have him reading to me while I'm busy about. If he doesn't know a word, he can spell it, and then I shall know what he's after—at least if it's not longer than Hawkie's tail."

Hawkie was a fine milking cow, with a bad temper, and a comical short tail. It had got chopped off by some accident when she was a calf.

"There's something else short about Hawkie—isn't there, Kirsty?" said my father.

"And Mrs. Mitchell," I suggested, thinking that I would help Kirsty see my father's meaning.

"Come, come, young gentleman! We don't want your remarks," said my father pointedly.

"Why, Papa, you told me so yourself, just before we came up."

"Yes, I did. But I did not mean you to repeat it. What if Kirsty were to go and tell Mrs. Mitchell what I said about her temper?"

Kirsty made no attempt to say a word. She knew well enough that my father knew there was no such danger. She only laughed. And seeing Kirsty satisfied, I joined in the laugh.

The result was that before many weeks were over, Allister and wee Davie were Kirsty's pupils also, Allister learning to read, and wee Davie learning to sit still, which was the hardest task within his capacity. They were free to come with me or stay at home. But they were not free to leave if they did come.

It soon became a regular thing. Every morning in summer we might be seen perched on a bench under one of the tiny windows in that delicious brown light which you seldom find except in an old clay-floored cottage. In the winter we seated ourselves round the fire. It was delightful to us boys! It would have been amusing to anyone to see how Kirsty behaved when Mrs. Mitchell came for a visit during lesson hours. She recognized her step and would dart to the door. Not once at such a time did she permit her to enter. She was like a hen with her chickens.

"No, you'll not come in just now, Mrs. Mitchell," she would say as the housekeeper attempted to pass. "You know we're busy."

"I want to know how they're getting on."

"You can test them at home," Kirsty would answer.

We always laughed at the idea of our reading to Mrs. Mitchell. Once I believe she heard the laugh, for she instantly walked away, and I do not remember that she ever came again when we were there.

43

—

THE DELIGHTS
OF COUNTRY

With Kirsty teaching us we were more than ever at the farm now. During the summer, from the time we got up and left it in the morning till we came back to go to bed, we seldom even approached the manse.

I have heard it hinted that my father neglected us. But that can hardly be, seeing that his word was law to us, and now I regard his memory as the symbol of complete and total love. My elder brother Tom always ate with our father, and sat doing his lessons in Father's study. But my father did not mind us younger ones running wild, so long as there was Kirsty to run to.

And all the men about the farm were also not only friendly to us, but careful and protective of us. No doubt we were a little wild, very different than city-bred children who are washed and dressed every time they go out for a walk. To us such a thing would have not merely been a hardship, but an indignity.

To be free was our whole idea of a perfect existence.

But a stern rebuke or word of discipline from my father was awful indeed if he found even the youngest guilty of untruth or cruelty or injustice. He would only smile at all kinds of escapades

and scrapes we got ourselves into when they did not involve dis-
obedience or disrespect to any creature. Except indeed there was
too much danger, and then he would speak a word to warn or limit
us.

A town boy or girl might wonder what we could find to do all
day long. But the fact is, almost everything was an amusement and
a delight to us. Since we could not participate in the work of the
farm that was going on, we generally managed to invent something
to do alongside it.

But you must not think of our farm as at all like some great
modern farm, for there was nothing done by machinery on the
place. There may be great pleasure in watching machine operations,
but surely none to equal the pleasure we had.

If there had been a steam engine to plough my father's fields,
how could we have ridden home on its back in the evening? To ride
the horses home from the plough was a triumph. Had there been
a threshing machine, could its pleasures have been comparable to
that of lying in the straw and watching the grain dance from the
sheaves under the skilful flails of the two strong men who beat
them? There was a winnowing machine, but quite a tame one, for
I could drive its wheel myself, and at the same time watch the storm
of chaff driven like drifting snowflakes from its wide mouth.

In the meantime, the oat grain was flowing in a silent slow
stream from the shelving hole in the other side, and the wind
rushed through the opposite doors of it, catching at the expelled
chaff, and carrying it yet farther. I can see old Eppie now, filling
her sack with what the wind blew her. The poor neighbor woman
was not after the grain. She wanted the fresh springy chaff to fill
her bed with. On it she would sleep as warm and sound and dry
and comfortable as her rheumatism would let her. For comfort is
on the inside more than the outside, and goose down, as soft and
cozy as it is, has less to do with comfort than most people imagine.
How I wish all the poor people in the great cities could have good
chaff beds to lie upon!

There are so many more machines nowadays than we had then.
I saw one going in the fields the other day. I could not even guess
what it was used for! Strange, wild-looking, mad machines that go
growling and snapping and clinking and clattering over the fields.

It seems to an old boy like me as if all the sweet poetic twilight of things are vanishing from the country. But then I must remind myself that God is not going to sleep, and the children of the earth are his, and he will see that their imaginations and feelings have food enough and plenty to spare. This is his business, not ours. So the work must be done as well as it can. And there need be no fear of the poetry.

I mentioned the pleasure of riding the horses, that is, the work-horses. Allister and I began to ride on them as far back as I can remember. First of all, we were allowed to take them at watering time, watched by one of the men, from the stable to the long trough that stood under the water pump. The horses would walk hurriedly to the trough, stop suddenly, and then drop head and neck and shoulders like a certain toy bird we had. Every time it caused us young riders a fear of falling over and down their necks into the trough of water. They would drink and drink until suddenly again they pulled up, and away with a quick refreshed stride they would trot toward the paradise of their stalls. Now came for us the fearful pass of the stable door, for they never stopped, but walked right in without thinking of us at all. There was just room, by stooping low, to clear the top of the door.

As we improved in our riding, we would go out in the fields and ride the horses home from the pasture where they were fastened by chains to short stakes of iron driven into the earth. There was more adventure in this, for not only was the ride longer, but the horses were more frisky and would sometimes set off at a gallop. Then again the chief danger was the door, for if they dashed in, our knees would be knocked against the posts and our heads against the lintels, for we only had halters to hold them with.

It was my father's desire that we should not be allowed a saddle until we could ride well on the bare back. It was a whole year before I was permitted to mount his little black riding mare called Missy. She was old, it is true, but if she felt even the slightest weight on her back, she instantly fancied herself young again and would dart off like the wind. When I was older and she was used to me—and she was older still and not so frolicsome—I would clamber upon her back and lie there reading my book, while she plucked on and ground and mashed away at the grass as if nobody were near her.

And then if nothing else was found to do, we could always go to the field where the cattle were grazing. Oh, the rich hot summer afternoons among the grass and the clover, the little lamb daisies, and the big horse daisies, with the cattle feeding so contentedly! Every once in a while one would stray to the grain field nearby, or the turnip patch, only to be called back by stern shouts from the cowherd. And if his shouts didn't bring them back, he would chase the stray cows down with his hefty stick.

Even in the cold days of spring, when the cattle were allowed to revel again in the growing green grass and daisies, there was pleasure to be found. The company and mischief of the cowherd constantly kept our lives interesting. He was a freckle-faced, white-haired boy of ten. I forget his real name: we always called him Turkey because his nose was the color of a turkey's egg.

Who but Turkey knew mushrooms from toadstools? Who but Turkey could find earth nuts? Who but Turkey knew the sound and the look and the nest of every bird in the country? Who but Turkey, with his little whip and its lash of brass wire, would stand and face the angriest bull in all Scotland?

In our eyes Turkey was a hero. Who but Turkey could discover the nests of the hens that had eluded Kirsty? And who so well as he could roast the egg with which she always rewarded such a discovery? Who could rob a wild bees' nest like Turkey? And who could be more fair in distributing the luscious prize? His accomplishments were too innumerable to recount. Short of flying, we younger boys believed him capable of everything imaginable.

What made him all the more dear to us was that neither he nor Mrs. Mitchell liked each other. The enmity between them came about in this way.

The cow Hawkie was a good milker, and therefore of necessity a big eater. Yet she was often tempted by an unnatural appetite for things altogether inedible. When she found a piece of an old shoe, for instance, in the field, she would go on the whole morning or afternoon chewing and chewing on it, even though there was no possible hope of digesting it. Turkey therefore had to keep watch on such occasions to make her drop the delicious mouthful and return to feeding upon the grass. When he failed, there was no way his inattention could not be discovered, for the near-empty milk pail would that same evening or next morning reveal the fact to Kirsty's watchful eyes. Without a stomach full of good grass, Hawkie could produce little milk.

But Hawkie's morbid craving was not limited to old shoes. One day when the cattle were feeding close to the manse, she found Mrs. Mitchell's best cap on the holly hedge where it had been laid out to bleach in the sun. It was a tempting morsel—and even more able to be chewed to bits than shoe leather. In the meantime, Mrs. Mitchell had gone for another load of linen which she was drying on the hedge. She arrived back only in time to see the end of one of the long strings of her cap gradually disappearing into Hawkie's mouth on its way after the rest.

With a wild cry of despair she flew at Hawkie. She grabbed hold of the string and pulled from the cow's throat the wet, messy wad of chewed-up cap. Turkey had come running up at her cry, and now he received the slimy and sloppy thing full across the face. But this was not all. For the next instant Mrs. Mitchell flew at him in her fury and boxed his ears soundly before he could recover himself enough to run for it. This treatment made Turkey into her enemy before he even knew that we too had plenty of reasons for disliking her. Ever after, he freely expressed his opinion. He said she was as bad as she was ugly, and always spoke of her as the old witch.

But what brought Turkey and us together more than anything else was that he was as fond of Kirsty's stories as we were. In the winter especially we would sit together in the evening, as I have already said, round her fire, with the great pot full of the most delicious potatoes, while Kirsty knitted away vigorously at her stockings, and kept a sort of time to her story with the sound of her needles. When the story dragged, the needles went slower. In the more exciting passages they would become invisible for swiftness, except for a certain shimmering flash hovering about her fingers. But as the story approached some crisis, their motion would become either perfectly frantic or else cease altogether. When they ceased, we knew that something awful indeed was at hand.

In my next chapter I will give a sample of her stories.

CHAPTER
ELEVEN

SIR WORM WYMBLE

It was a snowy evening in the middle of winter. Kirsty had promised to tell us the tale of the armed knight who lay in stone upon the tomb in the church. But the snow was so deep that Mrs. Mitchell had refused to let the little ones go out all day. She was always glad when nature gave her the power to exercise her authority in some way disagreeable to us. And she was not about to let us walk up to the farmhouse in this weather now that evening was falling.

Therefore, when the darkness began to grow thick enough, Turkey and I went prowling and watching about the manse until we found an opportunity when she was out of the way. That very moment we darted into the nursery, which was on the ground floor. I picked up wee Davie, and Turkey caught up Allister. We hoisted them on our backs and rushed from the house.

It *was* snowing! It came down in huge flakes. But although it was only half-past four o'clock, they did not show any whiteness, for there was no light to shine upon them. How the little ones did enjoy it, spurring their horses on with quiet laughter, telling us to hurry on lest the old witch should overtake us!

But it was hard work for one of the horses, and that one was me. Turkey went scampering away with his load as if it were nothing. But wee Davie pulled so hard with his little arms around my neck, especially when he was bobbing up and down to urge me on, half in delight, half in terror, that he nearly choked me. And all the while I knew that if I went one foot off the hardly recognizable beaten path, I would sink deep in the fresh snow.

"Doe on, doe on, Yanal!" cried Davie. And Yanal did his very best. But I was only halfway to the farm when Turkey came bounding back to take Davie from me. In a few moments more we had shaken the snow off our shoes and off Davie's back, and were standing around Kirsty's fire.

Kirsty seated herself on one side with Davie on her lap. We other three got our chairs as near her as we could, with Turkey, as the valiant man of the party, farthest from the center of safety, namely Kirsty, who was at the same time to be the source of all the delightful horror.

I may as well say that I do not believe Kirsty's tale had any true historical connection with Sir Worm Wymble, if that was in fact anything like the name of the dead knight in the church. What she told us was an old Highland legend, which she added to with the flowers of her own Celtic imagination, and then put around the form so familiar to us from Sunday to Sunday.

"There is a pot in the Highlands," began Kirsty, "not far from our house, at the bottom of a little glen. It is not very big, but fearfully deep, so deep that they say there is no bottom to it."

"An iron pot, Kirsty?" asked Allister.

"No, goosey," answered Kirsty. "A pot means a great hole full of water—black, black, and deep, deep."

"Oh!" remarked Allister, and was silent.

"Well, in this pot there lived a kelpie."

"What's a kelpie, Kirsty?" again interrupted Allister. In general he always asked all the necessary questions, and at least as many that were unnecessary.

"A kelpie is an awful creature that eats people."

"But what is it like, Kirsty?"

"It's something like a horse, with a head like a cow."

"How big is it? As big as Hawkie?"

"Bigger than Hawkie. Bigger than the biggest ox you ever saw."

"Does it have a big mouth?"

"Yes, a terrible mouth."

51

"With teeth?"

"Not many, but dreadfully big ones."

"Oh!"

"Well, there was a shepherd by the name of MacQueen many years ago who lived not far from the pot. He was the kind of man who knew all about kelpies and brownies and fairies. And he put a branch of the rowan tree, with the red berries in it, over the door of his cottage so that the kelpie could never come in.

"Now the shepherd had a very beautiful daughter—so beautiful that the kelpie wanted very much to eat her. I suppose he had lifted up his head out of the pot one day and seen her go past. But he could not come out of the pot except after the sun was down."

"Why?" asked Allister.

"I don't know. That's just the way kelpies do. His eyes couldn't stand the light, I suppose. But he could see in the dark quite well. And one night the girl woke up suddenly and saw his great huge head looking in at her window."

"But how could she see him when it was dark?" said Allister.

"His eyes were flashing so that they lighted up all his head," answered Kirsty.

"But he couldn't get in?"

"No, he couldn't get in. He was only looking in, and thinking how much he would like to eat her. So in the morning she told her father. And her father was very frightened and told her she must never be out one moment after the sun was down. And for a long time the girl was very careful. And she had need to be, for the creature never made any noise, but came up as quiet as a shadow.

"However, one afternoon she had gone to meet her lover a little way down the glen. They had talked with each other for so long, about one thing and another, that the sun was almost set before she realized how late it was. She said good night at once, and ran for home.

"Now she could not reach home without passing the pot, and just as she passed it, she saw the last sparkle of the sun as he went down."

"I should think she ran!" remarked our mouthpiece, Allister.

"She did run," said Kirsty. "She had just got past the awful black

52

water, which was terrible enough day or night without such a beast in it, when—"

"But there *was* a beast in it," said Allister.

"When," Kirsty went on without heeding him, "she heard a great *whish* of water behind her. That was the water tumbling off the beast's back as he came up from the bottom of the deep pool!

"If she ran before, she flew now. And the worst of it was that she couldn't hear him behind her so as to tell how close he was. He might be just opening his mouth to take her any moment. At last she reached the door to their cottage. Her father had gone out looking for her and had left it wide open so she could run straight in. But all the breath was out of her body, and just the moment she got inside she fell down."

Here Allister jumped from his seat, clapping his hands and crying, "Then the kelpie didn't eat her!"

"No. But as she fell, one foot was left outside the doorway so that the rowan branch could not take care of it. The beast laid hold of the foot with his great mouth in order to drag her out of the cottage and then eat her whenever he pleased."

Here Allister's face was a picture to behold! His hair was almost standing on end, his mouth open, and his face as white as my paper.

"Hurry, Kirsty," said Turkey, "or Allister will go into a fit."

"But her shoe came off in his mouth, and she drew her foot past the threshold and was safe."

Allister's hair went back down. He drew in a deep breath and sat down again. But Turkey must have been a very wise or a very unimaginative Turkey, for here he broke in.

"I don't believe a word of it, Kirsty."

"What!" said Kirsty. "You don't believe it!"

"No. She just lost her shoe in the mud."

"And the sound from the pot?"

"It was some wild duck in the water, and there was no beast after her. She never saw it, you know."

"She saw it look in at her window."

"Yes. And that was in the middle of the night. I've seen as much myself when I woke up in the middle of the night and my brain was playing tricks on me. I once thought a rat was a tiger."

Kirsty was looking angry, and her needles were going even faster than when she was approaching the climax of the story.

"Hold your tongue, Turkey," I said, "and let us hear the rest of the story."

But Kirsty kept her eyes on her knitting, and did not start up again.

"Is that all, Kirsty?" asked Allister.

Still Kirsty returned no answer. She needed all her force to overcome the anger she was busy keeping down. But after a few moments she began again as if she had never stopped and nothing had been said, only her voice trembled a little at first.

"Her father came home soon afterward in great distress. There he found her lying just within the door. His anger was immediately aroused, but more at her lover than the beast. He did not have any objection to her going to meet him, for they were both of the blood of the MacLeods."

This was in fact Kirsty's own clan. "But why was he angry with the gentleman?" asked Allister.

"Because he liked her company better than he loved her whole person," said Kirsty. "At least that was what the shepherd said, and that he ought to have had sense enough to see her safely home himself. But the shepherd didn't know that MacLeod's father had threatened to kill him if he ever spoke to the girl again."

"But why?" I said.

"Because he was a gentleman, and he didn't want his son having to do with a mere shepherd's daughter, even if she was a MacQueen and a member of the same clan."

"But I thought this story was about Sir Worm Wymble, not Mr. MacLeod," said Allister.

"And I will tell you how he got his new name," returned Kirsty, "if you will give me time. He wasn't Sir Worm Wymble then. His name was . . ."

Here she paused a moment and looked full at Allister. "His name was Allister—Allister MacLeod."

"Allister!" exclaimed my brother, repeating the name as an incredible coincidence.

"Yes, Allister," said Kirsty. "There's been many an Allister, and not all of them MacLeods, that did what they ought to do, and didn't know what fear was. And you'll be another such brave one, my bonny Allister," she added, stroking the boy's hair.

Allister's face beamed with pleasure. It was a long time before he asked another question.

"Well, as I say," resumed Kirsty, "the old shepherd was very angry, and told his daughter she could never go and meet Allister again. But the girl said she ought to go once more and let him know why she could not come anymore. And so he let her go to see him once more, and she told him all about it.

"Allister said nothing much right then. But the next day he came striding up to the cottage, right at dinnertime, with his claymore sword hanging from his hip on one side, and his long knife called a dirk hanging from the other, and his little skene dhu in his high sock. And he was grand to see—such a big strong gentleman! And he came striding up to the cottage in his kilt where the shepherd and his daughter were sitting having their dinner."

" 'Angus MacQueen,' he said, 'I understand the kelpie in the pot has been rude to your Nelly. I am going to kill him.'

" 'How will you do that, sir?' asked Angus, not altogether in a pleasant tone, for he was still angry with young MacLeod.

" 'Here's a claymore,' said Allister, 'and here's a shield made out of the hide of old Rasay's black bull, and here's my dirk made of a foot and a half of an old Andrew Ferrara sword, and here's a skene dhu that's so sharp I could drive it through your door, Mr. Angus. And so we're well fitted, I hope, to go after the beast.'

" 'Not at all,' said Angus, who I told you was a wise and knowing man. 'Not one bit. The kelpie's hide is thicker than three bull hides, and none of your weapons would do more than mark it.'

" 'What am I to do then, Angus, for I have to kill him somehow?'

" 'I'll tell you what to do, but it needs a brave man to do it.'

" 'And do you think I'm not brave enough for it?'

" 'I know one thing you're not brave enough for.'

" 'And what's that?' asked Allister.

" 'You're not brave enough to marry my girl in the face of the clan, knowing that she's only the daughter of a simple shepherd,' said Angus. 'But you shall not go on seeing her as you have. If my Nelly's good enough for you to talk to in the glen, she's good enough to lead into the hall before ladies and gentlemen.'

"Then Allister's face grew very red, but with shame rather than anger. He held his head down before the old man, but only for a few moments. When he lifted it again, it was pale, not with fear but with resolution, for he had made up his mind like a gentleman.

" 'Mr. Angus MacQueen,' he said, 'will you give me your daughter to be my wife?'

" 'If you kill the kelpie, I will,' answered Angus, for he knew that the man who could do that would be worthy of the shepherd's Nelly."

"But what if the kelpie ate him?" suggested Allister.

"Then he'd have to go without the girl," said Kirsty. "But," she resumed, "there's always some way of doing a difficult thing. And Allister, the gentleman, had Angus, the shepherd, to teach him.

"So Angus took Allister down to the pot, and there they began with their plan. They tumbled great stones together, and set them up in two rows at a little distance from each other, making a lane between the rows big enough for the kelpie to walk in. If the kelpie heard them, he could not see them, and they took care to get into the cottage before it was dark, for they could not finish their preparations in one day.

"They sat up all night, and saw the huge head of the beast looking in at the windows. As soon as the sun was up, they set to work again, and finished the two rows of stones all the way from the pot to the top of the little hill where the cottage stood. Next, they gathered a quantity of brushwood and peat and piled it in the end of the avenue next to the cottage. Then Angus went and killed a little pig and dressed it ready for cooking.

" 'Now you go down to my brother Hamish,' he said to Mr. MacLeod. 'He's a carpenter, you know, and you ask him to lend you his longest wimble.' "

"What's a wimble?" asked little Allister.

"A wimble is a long tool, like an auger, for boring into things, with a cross handle, with which you turn it like a screw. And Allister ran and fetched it, and got back only half an hour before the sun went down. They put Nelly into the cottage and shut the door. They had built up a great heap of stones behind the brushwood so the kelpie would have no means of escape except between the avenue of stones. And now they lighted the brushwood and put down the pig to roast by the fire. They laid the long metal end of the wimble in the fire halfway up to the handle. Then they laid themselves down behind the heap of stones and waited.

"By the time the sun was out of sight, the smell of the roasting pig had got down the avenue to the side of the pot, just where the kelpie always came out. He smelled it the moment he put his head up out of the water, and he thought it smelled so nice that he would go and see where it was. As soon as he got up on the land he was between the two walls of stones, but he never thought of that, for to the pig it was the straight way. So up the avenue he came, and since it was dark and his big soft webbed feet made no noise, the men could not see him until he came into the light of the fire.

" 'There he is!' cried Allister.

" 'Hush!' said Angus. 'He can hear well enough.'

"So the beast came on. Now Angus had meant that the kelpie should be busy with the pig before Allister attacked him. But that he should have the pig was a pity, Allister thought. So he put out his hand and got hold of the handle of the wimble and drew it gently out of the fire. The wimble was so hot that the metal turned white as the whitest moon you ever saw. The pig was so hot also that the brute was afraid to touch it, and before he ever even put his nose to it, Allister thrust the wimble into the kelpie's hide, behind his left shoulder, and bored away with all his might to screw the hot weapon into the creature's flesh.

"The kelpie gave a hideous roar, and turned away to run from the wimble. But he could not get past the row of stones, and he had to turn right around in the narrow space before he could run.

"Allister, however, could run as well as the kelpie, and he hung on to the handle of the wimble, giving it another turn at every chance as the beast went floundering on back toward the water, so that before he reached the pot the wimble had reached his heart, and the kelpie fell dead on the edge of the pot.

"Then the shepherd and Allister went home, and when the pig was properly done they had it for supper. And Angus gave Nelly to Allister, and they were married and lived happily ever after."

"But didn't Allister's father kill him?"

"No. He thought better of it. He was very angry for a while, but he got over it in time. And Allister became a great man, and because of what he had done, he was no longer called Allister MacLeod, but Sir Worm Wymble. And when he died," concluded Kirsty, "he was buried under the tomb in your father's church. And if you look close enough, you'll find a wimble carved on the stone, but I'm afraid it's worn out by this time."

CHAPTER
TWELVE

THE KELPIE

Silence followed the close of Kirsty's tale.
Wee Davie had taken no harm, for he was fast asleep with his head on her chest. Allister was staring into the fire, fancying he saw the twists of the wimble heating in it. Turkey was cutting at his stick with a blunt pocketknife, and a silent whistle on his puckered lips. I was sorry the story was over. At the same time I had already begun thinking that the next time I was in church, I would search for the wimble carved on the knight's tomb.

All at once came the sound of a latch lifted in vain, followed by a thundering at the outer door. Kirsty had prudently locked it earlier. Allister, Turkey, and I jumped to our feet in dread, Allister with a cry of dismay, Turkey grasping his stick.

"It's the kelpie!" cried Allister.

But the harsh voice of the old witch followed.

"Kirsty, Kirsty!" it cried. "Open this door at once."

"No, no, Kirsty!" I objected. "She'll shake wee Davie to bits and haul Allister through the snow."

Turkey thrust his poker into the fire. But Kirsty snatched it out, threw it down, and boxed his ears. He took her rough treatment with the pleasantest laugh in the world. Kirsty was no tyrant, so she could do as she pleased. She turned to us.

"Hush!" she said hurriedly, with a twinkle in her eye. "Hush—don't speak, wee Davie," she continued as she rose and carried him from the kitchen into the passage between it and the outer door. He was scarcely awake.

In that wide hallway stood a huge barrel which Kirsty had recently cleaned out. She gently set Davie down on the floor. Then she and Turkey lifted first me and popped me into it, and then Allister. We saw at once what she intended. Finally she took up wee Davie, told him to lie as still as a mouse, and then dropped him into our arms. I happened to find the open bunghole near my eye, and peeped out. The knocking at the outer door continued.

"Wait a bit, Mrs. Mitchell!" yelled Kirsty. "Wait till I get my potatoes off the fire."

As she spoke, she took the great iron pot in one hand and carried it to the door to pour away the water. When she unlocked and opened the door, I saw through my peep hole a lovely sight. The moon was shining and the snow was falling thick. In the midst of it stood Mrs. Mitchell, one mass of whiteness. She would have rushed straight in, but Kirsty's advance with the pot made her step aside. From behind Kirsty, Turkey slipped out and around the corner without being seen. There he stood watching, but busy at the same time making snowballs.

"And what may you please to want tonight, Mrs. Mitchell?" said Kirsty in her most friendly voice.

"What should I want but my poor children? They ought to have been in bed an hour ago. Really, Kirsty, you ought to have more sense at your years than to encourage any such goings-on."

"At my years!" returned Kirsty. She was about to give back a sharp retort, but she stopped herself. "Aren't they in bed then, Mrs. Mitchell?"

"You know well enough they are not."

"Poor things! I would recommend you put them to bed at once."

"So I will. Where are they?"

"Find them yourself, Mrs. Mitchell. You had better ask a kindly tongue to help you. I'm not going to do it."

They were standing just inside the door. Mrs. Mitchell took a step inside. I trembled. It seemed impossible she could not see me as well as I could see her. I had a vague feeling that by looking at her I would draw her eyes upon me. But I could not take my eyes from the hole. I was fascinated, and the nearer she came, the less could I keep from watching her. When she turned into the kitchen, it was a great relief. But it did not last for long, for she came out again in a moment, searching like a hound. She was taller than Kirsty, and by standing on her tiptoes could have looked right down into the barrel. She was approaching! Already her apron hid all other vision from my one eye, she was so close.

Suddenly came a whiz, a dull blow, and a shriek from Mrs. Mitchell.

The next moment my field of vision was open again, and I saw Mrs. Mitchell holding her head with both hands, and the face of Turkey grinning around the corner of the open door. He was trying to make her follow him, but she had been too much astonished by the snowball in the back of her neck even to look in the direction from which the blow had come. Turkey stepped out into the open and was just poising himself for the delivery of a second missile when she turned around and saw him.

The snowball missed her, and came with a great bang against the barrel. Wee Davie gave a cry of alarm. But there was no danger of our discovery now, for Mrs. Mitchell was off after Turkey. In a moment Kirsty lowered the barrel on its side, and we all crept out. I had wee Davie on my back in an instant, while Kirsty caught up Allister, and we were off for the manse.

As soon as we had left the yard, however, we met Turkey out of breath. He had given Mrs. Mitchell the slip and left her searching the barn for him. He took Allister from Kirsty, and we sped away, for it was all downhill now.

When Mrs. Mitchell got back to the farmhouse, Kirsty was busy as if nothing had happened. After a fruitless search, the woman returned to the manse to find us all snug in bed with the door locked. After what had passed about the school, Mrs. Mitchell did not dare make any disturbance.

From that night she always went by the name of *the Kelpie*.

Chapter Thirteen

ANOTHER KELPIE

During the summer we all slept in a large attic room under the wide sloping roof. It had a dormer window above the eaves.

One day there was something doing about the ivy, which covered all the gable and half the front of the house. The ladder they had been using was left leaning against the back. It reached a little above the eaves, right under the dormer window.

That night I could not go to sleep. On such occasions I used to go wandering about the upper part of the house. I believe the servants thought I walked in my sleep, but it was not so, for I always knew what I was about well enough. And such times gave me a pleasure arising from a sort of sense of protected danger.

On that memorable night when I awoke in the barn and later found myself alone in the starry loneliness, I had been as it were naked to all the silence, alone in the vast universe, which kept looking at me full of something it knew but would not speak.

Now, when wandering about sleepless, I could gaze, as from a nest of safety, out upon the beautiful fear outside. I would go from window to window in the middle of the night, gazing at one time into a blank darkness out of which came raindrops or hailstones against the panes of the glass, or another into the deeps of the blue night sky with gold around its northern edges, or still another into the mysteries of soft clouds gathered about the moon, thinking out her light over their shining and shadowy folds.

As I have said, this was one of those nights on which I could not sleep. It was the summer after the winter story of the kelpie, I think, but the years of the past grow confusing in the continuous *now* of childhood.

The night was hot. My little brothers were sleeping loudly, as wee Davie called *snoring*, and a huge moth was caught within my curtains somewhere and kept on fluttering and whirring. I got up and went to the window.

It was such a night! The moon was full, but rather low and looked as if she were thinking: "Nobody is paying any attention to me. I may as well go to bed." All the top of the sky was covered with clouds, lying like milky ripples on a blue sea, and the stars shot through them here and there like the little rays of sparkling diamonds. There was no awfulness about it, as on the night when the black sky stood over me in empty nothingness. The clouds were like the veil that hid the terrible light in the Holy of Holies—a curtain of God's love to make his children able to bear it.

My eyes fell upon the top rungs of the ladder leaning up against the back of the house, which rose above the edge of the roof like an invitation. I opened the window, crept through, and, holding on by the ledge, let myself down over the slates, feeling with my feet for the top of the ladder.

In a moment I was upon it. Down I went. How tender to my bare feet was the cool grass when I lighted upon it. I looked up. The dark wall of the house rose above me. I could go back up to the room when I pleased. There was no hurry. I would walk about a little. I would go a little farther from my place of refuge, nibble at the danger, as it were—a danger which existed only in my imagination. I went outside the high holly hedge, and even though I was still close to it, now the house was hidden from my view. A grassy field was in front of me, and just beyond the field rose the farm buildings.

Why shouldn't I run across it and wake Turkey?

Off I went like a shot. The expectation of a companion to share my middle-of-the-night delight overcame all the remnants of lingering fear. I knew the door had only one bolt, and that a manageable one, for Turkey slept in a little wooden room partitioned off from a loft in the barn. He had to climb up to it by a ladder.

The only fearful part was the crossing of the barn floor, for it would be very dark. But I was man enough for that!

I reached the yard of the farm, then crossed it in safety. I searched for the key to the barn. It was always left in a hole in the wall by the door. I found it easily, turned it in the lock, crept inside, and crossed the floor as fast as the darkness would allow me. With outstretched groping hands I found the ladder, climbed up, and in a few seconds was standing beside Turkey's bed.

"Turkey! Turkey! Wake up!" I cried. "It's such a beautiful night! It's a shame to lie there sleeping."

Turkey's answer was immediate. He was wide awake and out of bed with all his wits by him in a moment.

"Shh . . . shh!" he whispered, "or you'll wake Oscar."

Oscar was the sheep dog, a collie, who slept in a kennel in the corn yard. He was not much of a watchdog. There was not much to watch, and he knew it, and therefore slept as soundly as a human child. But he was the most knowing of dogs. Meanwhile Turkey was getting dressed.

"Never mind your clothes, Turkey," I said. "There's nobody up."

Turkey was willing enough to be spared the trouble, and so followed me down the ladder and out in just his shirt. But once we were out in the yard, instead of finding peace and contentment in the sky and the moon as I did, the practical Turkey wanted to know what we were going to do.

"It's not a bad sort of night," he said. "What shall we do with it?" He was always wanting to do something.

"Oh, just look about a bit I suppose."

"You didn't hear robbers, did you?" he asked.

"Oh no! I couldn't sleep, so I got down the ladder and came to wake you—that's all."

"Let's go for a walk, then," he said.

Now that I was with Turkey, there was scarcely more terror in the night than in the day. So I agreed at once. We had no shoes on, but that was of no consequence to Scotch boys. We often went barefooted in summer.

As we left the barn, Turkey had grabbed his little whip. He was never to be seen without either that or his club—what we called the stick he carried when he was herding the cattle. Since he had the whip, I begged him to give me his club. He ran and fetched it. And thus armed, we set out for nowhere in the middle of the night.

My imagination was full of fragmentary notions of adventure, which were mostly made up of shadows from *Pilgrim's Progress*. I set my club on my shoulder, trying to persuade myself that the unchristian weapon had been won from some pagan giant. But Turkey was far better armed with his lash of wire than I was with the club. His little whip was like a fearful weapon in the hand of some stalwart knight.

We took our way toward the nearest hills, hardly even thinking of where we were going. I guess that the story of the kelpie must have been working in Turkey's brain that night in spite of his unbelief. For after we had walked for a mile or more along the road and had arrived at the foot of a wooded hill, he turned into the hollow of a broken trail which soon lost itself in moorland. It was becoming plain to me now that Turkey had some goal or other in his mind. But I followed his leading, and asked no questions.

All at once he stopped, pointed a few yards in front of him, and said, "Look, Ranald!"

The moon was behind the hill, and the night was so dim that I had to keep looking for several moments before I discovered he was pointing to the dull gleam of a pool of very black water. It seemed horrible! I felt my flesh creep the instant I saw it. It lay in a hollow, left by the digging out of peats, into which the water had drained from the surrounding bog.

My heart sank with fear! The dark glimmer of its surface was bad enough, but who could tell what lay in its unknown depths?

As I gazed, almost paralyzed, a huge dark figure suddenly rose up on the opposite side of the pool. For one moment Turkey's skepticism failed him.

"The kelpie! The kelpie!" he cried, and turned and ran.

I was after him before the words were out of his mouth, following as fast as feet utterly unconscious of the ground they sped over could bear me. But we had not gone many yards before a great roar filled the silent air behind us. I was terrified! Yet almost the same moment Turkey slowed his pace and burst into a fit of laughter.

"It's nothing but Bogbonny's bull, Ranald!" he cried.

Kelpies were unknown creatures to Turkey, and for him a bull was no worse than a dog or a sheep or any other domestic animal. I did not share his composure, however, and didn't let up my pace till I caught up to him.

"Though he is a rather mean one," he went on the instant I joined him, "we'd better make for the hill."

Another roar behind us gave renewed enthusiasm to our speed. We could not have been in better fitness for running. But it was all uphill. And had it not been for the fact that the distance between us and the animal was boggy so that he had to go a long way around to reach us, one of us at least would have been in an evil case.

"He's caught sight of our shirts," said Turkey, panting as he ran, "and he wants to see what they are. But we'll be over the fence before he catches up with us."

I was running as fast as humanly possible just to barely keep up with him!

"I wouldn't mind for myself," Turkey went on. "I could dodge him well enough. But he might go after you, Ranald."

With fear and exhaustion I could not reply. Another bellow sounded out in the night. It was nearer! Before too many more moments we could hear the dull pounding of his hoofs on the soft dry ground as he galloped after us. But the dyke fence of dry stones and the larch wood on the other side were close at hand.

We reached the dyke. "Over with you, Ranald!" cried Turkey, as if with his last breath. Then he turned around. The brute was close behind him!

But I was so spent I could not climb the wall of rocks. And when I saw Turkey turn and face the bull, I turned too. We were now in the shadow of the hill, but I could just see Turkey lift his arm. A short sharp hiss, and a roar followed. The bull tossed his head as if in pain, left Turkey, and came toward me.

He could not charge at any great speed, for the ground was steep and uneven. I too had kept hold of my weapon, and although I was dreadfully frightened, I felt my courage rise at Turkey's success. I lifted my club in the hope that it might prove as good for the job as Turkey's whip.

It was well for me, however, that Turkey was too quick for the bull. He got between him and me, and a second stinging cut from the brass wire drew a second roar from his throat, and no doubt a second red stream from his nose, while my club fell on one of his horns with a bang which jarred my arm all the way to the elbow, and sent the weapon flying over the fence.

The animal turned tail for the moment—long enough to get us, given new life by our success, on the other side of the wall, where we crouched down so he could not see us. Turkey, however, kept looking up at the line of the wall against the sky. And as he looked, over came the nose of the bull within a yard of Turkey's head. Hiss went the little whip, and bellow went the bull.

"Get up among the trees, Ranald, just in case he comes over," whispered Turkey.

I obeyed and ran. But as he could see nothing of his foes, the animal had enough of it, and we heard no more of him.

After a while Turkey left his lair by the wall and joined me. We rested for a little, and then began to climb to the top of the hill. But we gave up the attempt after getting caught in some nasty bushes. In our condition, it was too dark for such a climb.

I started to grow sleepy, too, and began to think that I would like to exchange the hillside for my bed. Turkey made no objection, so we trudged home again, though not without many starts and jumps and quick glances to make sure the bull was neither after us on the road nor watching us from behind this bush or that little slope of hill.

Turkey never left me till he saw me safe up the ladder. Even, in fact, after I was in bed I spied his face peeping in at the window from the topmost part of it. By this time the east had begun to glow. But I was good and tired now. I fell asleep at once and never woke until Mrs. Mitchell pulled my clothes off me.

It was an indignity which I keenly felt, but did not yet know how to render impossible for the future.

Chapter Fourteen

WANDERING WILLIE

A t that time there were a good many beggars going about the country, who lived on the gifts from those kind to them. Among these were some half-witted persons that could not be relied upon, yet were seldom mischievous in any serious way. We were not much afraid of them, for the neighborhood of our home seemed to have a magic circle of safety around it, and we seldom roamed far beyond it.

There was, however, one occasional visitor of this class of beggars whom we were quite awed by. He was commonly called Wandering Willie. His approach to the manse was always announced by a wailful strain upon the set of bagpipes he had inherited from his father, formerly a piper to some Highland nobleman. At least so it was said.

Willie never went anywhere without his bagpipes, and was more attached to them than to any living creature. He played them well, too, though in what corner he kept the amount of intellect necessary to have mastered them was a puzzle. Probably his wits had not left him until after he had learned to play. However this may be, Willie could certainly play the pipes, and was a great favorite with children because of it, even though they were a little afraid of him as well.

Whether it was from our Highland blood or from Kirsty's stories, I do not know, but we were always delighted when the far-off sound of his pipes reached us. Little Davie would dance and shout with glee. Even the Kelpie, Mrs. Mitchell, did not seem to mind Wandering Willie. She was so considerate to him, in fact, that Turkey— who was always trying to account for things—declared his belief that Willie must be Mrs. Mitchell's brother, only she was ashamed and wouldn't admit it. I do not believe he had the smallest atom of evidence, which made the notion a bold one worthy of its inventor. One thing we all knew, that she would fill the canvas bag he carried by his side with any broken scraps she could gather, would give him as much milk to drink as he pleased, and would speak more kindly to him than any of the rest of us.

It is impossible to describe what Willie looked like. His clothes were a conglomeration of whatever came to him, which he would wear *all* at any whim and in any combination. He loved to pin on himself whatever bright-colored cotton handkerchiefs he could get hold of. With one of these behind and one in front, spread out across his back and chest, he always looked like an ancient herald coming with a message from a knight or nobleman. His costumes were so peculiar that I could never tell whether he had started with kilt or trousers, and had then built it up from there. To his tattered garments were attached bits of old ribbon, colored rags which he added to his pipes wherever there was room, and you can imagine that he looked like a walking assortment of flags and pendants—a moving tree of rags, out of which came the screaming chant and drone of his instrument. When he danced he was like a whirlwind that had caught up the contents of an old clothesline.

It is no wonder that he should have produced in our minds an indescribable mixture of awe and delight—awe, because no one could tell what he might do next, and delight because of his oddity, agility, and music.

The first sensation upon seeing him was always a slight fear, which gradually wore off as we became accustomed to his strangeness all over again. Before the visit was over, wee Davie would be playing with the dangles of his pipes, and laying his ear to the bag, thinking that was where the music came from ready-made. Willie was particularly fond of David, and tried to make himself agreeable to him in a hundred grotesque ways. The awe, however, was constantly renewed when he was gone, partly by the threats of the Kelpie, that, if so and so, she would give one of us to Wandering Willie to take away with him.

One day in early summer, after I had begun to go to school, I came home as usual at five o'clock, to find the manse in great commotion. Wee Davie had disappeared. They were looking for him everywhere without success. Already all the farm buildings had been thoroughly searched.

An awful horror fell upon me, and the most frightful ideas of Davie's fate arose in my mind. I remember giving a howl of dismay the moment I heard of the catastrophe. I immediately received a sound box on the ear from Mrs. Mitchell. But I was too miserable to show any resentment. So I sat down on the grass and cried.

In a few minutes my father, who had been away visiting some of his parishioners, rode up on his little black mare. Mrs. Mitchell hurried to meet him, wringing her hands and crying:

"Oh, sir! oh, sir! Davie's away with Wandering Willie!"

This was the first I had heard of Willie in connection with the affair. My father turned pale but kept perfectly quiet.

"Which way did he go?" he asked. Nobody knew. "How long has he been gone?"

"About an hour and a half, I think," said Mrs. Mitchell.

To me the news was some relief. Now I could at least do something. I left the group and hurried away to find Turkey. Except for my father, I trusted more in Turkey than in anyone alive.

I ran to a bit of high ground near the manse and looked all about until I found where the cattle were feeding that afternoon. Then I darted off at full speed. They were some distance from home, and when I got there I found that Turkey had heard nothing of the mishap. Once I had told him the dreadful news, he shouldered his club and said:

"The cows must look after themselves!"

With the words he set off at a good trot in the direction of a little rocky knoll in a hollow about half a mile away, which he knew to be a favorite haunt of Wandering Willie whenever he happened to be in our neighborhood. There were some stunted trees, gnarled and old, with very mossy trunks, growing on this knoll. The stones, too, had moss, and between them tall foxgloves, which were always in season. These flowers almost made me slightly afraid of the spot. For in that region they call them *Dead Man's Bells*, and I thought there was a murdered man buried somewhere nearby. I would not have wanted to be in that hollow alone even in the broad daylight. But with Turkey I would have gone at any hour, even without the impulse which now urged me to follow him at my best speed.

In no time at all Turkey was some distance ahead of me. He dropped to a walk and I saw him approach the knoll with some caution. I soon caught up with him.

"He's there, Ranald!" he said.

"Who. . .Davie?"

"I don't know about Davie, but Willie's there."

"How do you know?"

"I heard his bagpipes grunt. Perhaps Davie sat down on them."

"What shall we do, Turkey?" I said anxiously.

"If Willie has him," he returned, "he won't hurt him. But it might not be easy to get him away. We must creep up and see what can be done."

Half dead as some of the trees were, there were still enough leaves and brush about to hide Willie from our view, and Turkey hoped they would help to hide our approach as well. He got down on his hands and knees and crept toward the knoll. I followed his example, and found I could keep up with him better when crawling in four-footed fashion. When we reached the steep side of the top, we lay still and listened.

"He's there!" I cried in a whisper.

"Shh!" said Turkey. "I hear him. It's all right. We'll soon have ahold of him."

The weary whimper of a child worn out with hopeless crying reached our ears. Turkey immediately began to climb the remaining distance to the peak of the knoll.

"Stay where you are, Ranald," he said. "I can go up quieter than you." I obeyed. Cautious as if he were stalking a deer, he went the rest of the way up the hill, still on his hands and knees. I strained my eyes to watch his every motion. But when he was at the top he lay perfectly quiet, and continued in that position till I could stand it no longer, and crept up after him. When I came behind him, he looked around angrily and made a most emphatic contortion of his face. After that I dared not go the rest of the way with him, but lay trembling with expectation. The next moment I heard him call in a low whisper:

"Davie . . . Davie! Wee Davie!" There was no reply.

He called a little louder, trying to inch up to the loudness that would pierce to Davie's ears and not arrive at Wandering Willie's, who I presumed was a little farther away.

Turkey's tones grew louder and louder—but had not yet risen above a sharp whisper, when at length a small trembling voice cried "Turkey! Turkey!" in a tone of mingled hope and pain.

There was a sound in the bushes above me. I could see nothing. Then came a louder sound and a rush.

Turkey sprang to his feet and vanished! I followed.

Before I reached the top, there came a despairing cry from Davie, and a shout and a gabble of nonsense sounds from Willie. Then followed a louder shout and a louder gabble, mixed with a scream from the bagpipes, and an exulting laugh from Turkey.

All this passed in the moment I spent scrambling to the top of the knoll, the last bit of which was steep and difficult. I looked down into the hollow on the other side.

There was Davie alone in the thicket. Turkey was scuddling down the opposite slope with the bagpipes under his arm, and Wandering Willie was pursuing him in a foaming fury.

I ran down the knoll and caught Davie up in my arms, where he lay sobbing and crying, "Yanal! Yanal!"

I stood with him for a moment not knowing what to do. But I was resolved to fight tooth and nail if Willie should try to take him again. In the meantime, Turkey led Willie off toward the deepest of the boggy ground. Both of them were soon floundering in it, only that Turkey, being the lighter, had the advantage. When I saw them thus slowed down, I decided to make for home.

I got Davie on my back and slid down the farther side to avoid the bog. I had not gone far, however, before a howl from Willie made me aware that he had caught sight of us. Looking around, I saw him turn from chasing Turkey to come after us. Presently, however, he hesitated, then stopped. He began looking this way and that, and from one to the other of his treasures—Davie and the bagpipes—now both in evil hands.

His indecision would have appeared ludicrous to an observer, but to my thinking he made up his mind far too soon, for he chose to follow Davie. I ran my best in the very strength of despair for some distance. But very soon I saw that I had no chance of getting home before he would easily overtake us.

I set Davie down and told him to stay behind me. Then I turned around to face our foe!

Willie came on in fury, his rags fluttering like ten scarecrows as he waved his arms in the air and made wild gestures and grimaces and cries and curses. He was more terrible than the bull, and Turkey was behind him and could not help us!

I got myself ready to run my head into the pit of his stomach, hoping to be able to knock him off his feet. But that instant I saw Turkey running toward us at full speed, blowing the bagpipes as he ran. How he found breath to run and blow at the same time I could not understand!

Finally he put the bag under his arm, and the next moment came from it such a combination of screeching and grunting and howling that Wandering Willie, in the full flight of his rage, turned at the cries of his musical companion.

Then came Turkey's masterpiece!

He dashed the bagpipes on the ground and began kicking them in front of him like a ball, and the pipes cried out at every kick. If he had been trying to destroy them completely, he could not have treated them worse! It was no time for gentle measure: my life hung in the balance.

This was more than Willie could bear! He turned from us, and once again ran to rescue his pipes. When Willie had nearly overtaken him, Turkey gave them one last masterly kick, which sent them flying through the air. He caught them as they fell, then again ran off toward the bog. I hoisted Davie on my back and hurried with more haste than speed toward home.

What took place after I left them, I can only tell you what Turkey later told me, for I never looked behind me until I reached the little green lawn in front of the house. There I set Davie down and threw myself on the grass. I remember nothing more until I came to myself in bed.

When Turkey reached the bog and had again got Wandering Willie into the middle of it, he threw the bagpipes as far beyond him as he could, and then made his way out to one side. Willie followed the pipes, got them at last, held them up between him and the sky as if appealing to heaven against the cruelty, then sat down in the middle of the bog on a solitary hump of ground and cried like a child.

Turkey stood and watched him, at first with feelings of triumph, which slowly cooled down until finally they passed over into compassion, and he grew heartily sorry for the fellow.

After Willie had cried for a while, he took the instrument as if it had been the mangled corpse of his son, and proceeded to examine it. Turkey said he was certain none of the pipes were broken, but when at length Willie put the mouthpiece to his lips and began to blow into the bag, alas! it would hold no wind. He flung it from him in anger and cried again. Turkey left him crying in the middle of the bog. He said it was a pitiful sight.

It was a long time before Willie appeared in that part of the country again. But about six months afterward, some neighbors who had been to a fair twenty miles away told my father that they had seen him looking much as usual, and playing his pipes with more energy than ever. This was a great relief to my father, who could not bear the idea of the poor fellow's loneliness without his pipes, and had wanted very much to get them repaired for him.

But ever after that my father showed a great regard for Turkey. I heard him say once that if he had the chance, Turkey would have made a great general. Such a statement was hardly surprising to me. Yet he became as a result a still greater being in my eyes.

When I set Davie down, and fell myself on the grass, there was nobody near. Everyone was busy in a new search for Davie. My father had ridden off at once without even dismounting. But wherever he went asking, he failed to turn up so much as a single clue. It was twilight before he returned. How long, therefore, I lay upon the grass, I do not know. When I came to myself, I found a sharp pain in my side. No matter how I turned, there it was, and I could take in only a very short breath. I was in my father's bed, and there was no one in the room. I lay for some time in increasing pain, but in a little while my father came in, and then I felt that all was as it should be. Seeing me awake, he approached with an anxious face.

"Is Davie all right, Father?" I asked.

"He is quite well, Ranald, my boy. How do you feel yourself?"

"I've been asleep, Father."

"Yes, we found you on the grass, with Davie pulling at you and trying to wake you. He was crying, 'Yanal won't peak to me. Yanal! Yanal!' I am afraid you had a terrible run with him. Turkey, as you call him, told me all about it. That Turkey's a fine lad."

"Indeed he is, Father," I said with a gasp that gave away the suffering caused by the pain in my side.

"What is the matter, my boy?" he asked.

"I have *such* a pain in my side!"

"We must send for the old doctor."

The old doctor was a sort of demigod in the place. Everybody believed and trusted in him, and nobody could die in peace without him any more than without my father. I was delighted at the thought of being his patient. I can see him now in my imagination standing with his back to the fire, and taking his lancet from his pocket, while preparations were being made for bleeding me at the arm, which was a far commoner operation then than it is now.

That night I was delirious and haunted with bagpipes. Wandering Willie was nowhere in my dreams, but the atmosphere was full of bagpipes. It was an unremitting storm of bagpipes, coming at me from every direction, and all the while I was toiling along with little Davie on my back.

The next day I was a little better, but very weak, and it was several days before my strength returned. My father soon found it would not do to let Mrs. Mitchell attend to me, for I was always worse after she had been in the room for any length of time. So he got another woman to take Kirsty's duties, and set Kirsty up to nurse me. After that the illness became almost a luxury. And the growing better was pure enjoyment.

Once, when Kirsty was gone for a little while, Mrs. Mitchell brought me some gruel.

"The porridge tastes bad," I said.

"It's perfectly good, Ranald, and there's no use in complaining when everybody's trying to make you as comfortable as they can," said the Kelpie.

"Let me taste it," said Kirsty, who happened to enter the room that very moment. She did so, then exclaimed, "It's not fit for anybody to eat!" and carried it away. Mrs. Mitchell followed her with her nose horizontal.

Oh, what a delight was that first glowing afternoon when I was carried out to the field where Turkey was herding the cattle! I could not yet walk, from the soreness and unsteadiness in my legs. Kirsty set me down on a tartan blanket in the grass. The next moment, Turkey was standing by my side. He looked awfully big and portentously healthy! I wish I could give the conversation in the native Scottish dialect, for it loses much in translation.

"Eh, Ranald!" said Turkey, "you're not yourself."

"It's me, Turkey," I said, nearly crying with pleasure.

"Well," he returned, as if consoling me in some disappointment, "we'll have some fun yet."

"I'm frightened at the cows, Turkey. Don't let them come near me."

"That I won't," answered Turkey, waiving his club above his head to give me confidence. "I'll let them have it if they even look at you from between their ugly horns."

"Turkey," I said, for I had been thinking about the matter during my illness, "how did Hawkie behave while you were away with me—that day, you know?"

"She ate about half a rick of green corn," answered Turkey. "But she had the worst of it. She got sick from it. There she is—off to the turnips!"

He was after her with a shout and flourish! Hawkie heard him and obeyed, turning round on her hind legs with a sudden start. She knew from his voice that he was in a dangerously energetic mood.

"You'll be all right again soon," he said, coming quietly back to me. In the meantime, Kirsty had gone to the farmhouse, having given Turkey solemn orders to take care of me.

"Oh yes," I said, "I'm nearly well now, only my legs are weak."

"Will you come on my back?" he asked.

When Kirsty returned to take me home, there I was on Turkey's back, following the cows, riding him about wherever I chose. My horse was as obedient as a dog, or a horse, or a servant from love could possibly be.

From that day I recovered very rapidly.

CHAPTER
FIFTEEN
—

ELSIE DUFF

How all the boys and girls stared at me as I timidly entered the parish school one morning a week or two later about ten o'clock. There was a sense of importance over my entry from the distinction of having been so ill. As I have said, I had gone to school for some months before I was taken ill by the incident over Davie and Wandering Willie.

It was a very different affair from Dame Shand's tyrannical little kingdom. Here were boys of all ages, and girls too, ruled over by an energetic young man who was very enthusiastic about teaching. He spoke to me kindly the first day I went, and I was attached to him ever after—even when once he thought I had been guilty of an offense that was actually committed by my neighbor. He ordered me to the front with more severity than usual and told me to hold out my hand. The lash stung me dreadfully, but I was able to smile in his face in spite of it. I could not have done that had I been guilty.

The moment he saw me enter, the master came up to me and took me by the hand. He said he was glad to see me able to come to school again.

"You must try not to do too much at first," he added.

His words inspired me, and I worked hard. But before the morning was over I grew very tired and fell fast asleep with my head on the desk. I was told afterward that the master had kept one of my classmates from waking me, and told him to let me sleep.

When one o'clock came, the noise of dismissal for the two hours for dinner woke me up. I staggered out, still sleepy, and whom should I find watching for me by the doorpost but Turkey!

"Turkey!" I exclaimed, "what are you doing here?"

"I've put the cows up for an hour or two, for it was very hot," he said, "and Kirsty said I might come and carry you home."

He stooped down in front of me, and took me on his strong back. As soon as I was well settled, he turned his head toward me.

"Ranald," he said, "I would like to go have a visit with my mother. Will you come? There's plenty of time."

"Yes, Turkey," I answered. "I've never seen your mother."

He set off at a slow easy trot, taking me through street and lane until we arrived at a two-story house, where his mother lived in the attic. She was a widow and had only Turkey.

What a curious place her little garret was! The roof sloped down on one side to the very floor, and there was a little window in it, from which I could see away to the manse, a mile off, and far beyond it. Her bed stood in one corner. In another was a chest, which contained all her spare clothes, including Turkey's best garments, which he went home to put on every Sunday morning. In the little fireplace smoldered a fire of oak bark, which the tan yard gave to the poor for nothing.

Turkey's mother was sitting near the little window spinning. She was a thin, sad-looking woman, with loving eyes and slow speech.

"Johnnie!" she exclaimed, "what brings you here? And who's this you've brought with you?"

Instead of stopping her work as she spoke, she made her wheel go faster than before. I gazed with admiration at the continuous thread of wool that looked as if it were flowing out of her fingers toward the revolving spool.

"It's Ranald Bannerman," said Turkey quietly. "I'm his horse. I'm taking him home from the school. This is the first time he's been there since he was ill."

She relaxed her labor, until gradually the pieces of the spinning wheel slowed, and at last stood quite still. She rose.

"Come, Master Ranald, and sit down," she said. "You'll be tired of riding such a rough horse as that."

"No, indeed," I said. "Turkey is not a rough horse. He's the best horse in the world."

"He always calls me Turkey, Mother, because of my nose," said Turkey, laughing.

"And what brings you here?" asked his mother. "This is not on the road to the manse."

"I wanted to see if you were better, Mother."

"But what becomes of the cows?"

"Oh, they're safe enough! They know I'm here."

"Well, sit down and rest, both of you," she said, resuming her own seat at the spinning wheel. "I'm glad to see you, Johnnie, just so long as your work is not neglected. But I must go on with mine."

Turkey deposited me on his mother's bed, and sat down beside me.

"And how's your papa, the good man?" she asked me. I told her he was quite well.

"All the better that you're back from the edge of the grave, I don't doubt," she said.

I had never known before that I had been in any danger.

"It's been a difficult time for him, and you too," she added. "You must be a good son to him, Ranald, for he was greatly worried about you, they tell me."

Turkey said nothing. I was too much surprised to know what to say, for as often as my father had come into my room he had always looked cheerful. I had no idea that he was uneasy about me.

After a little more talk, Turkey rose and said we must be going.

"Well, Ranald," said his mother, "you must come and see me any time when you're tired at the school, so you can lie down and rest yourself a bit. Be a good lad, Johnnie, and mind your work."

"Yes, Mother, I'll try," answered Turkey cheerfully as he hoisted me once more upon his back. "Good-day, Mother," he added as we left the room.

I mention this little incident because it led to other things afterward. I rode home upon Turkey's back, and with my father's permission, instead of returning to school later that afternoon, spent the rest of the day in the fields with Turkey.

In the middle of the field where the cattle were that day, there was a large circular mound. I have often thought since that it must have been an ancient grave with dead men's bones in the middle of it, but no such suspicion had crossed my mind at that point in my young life. Its sides were rather steep and covered with lovely grass. On the side farthest from the manse, where there was no human dwelling to be seen, Turkey and I lay that afternoon in perfect bliss. My ecstasy was no doubt even greater because of the occasional thought of the hot, dusty classroom. A fitful little breeze, as if it was itself controlled by the influence of the heat, would wake up for a few moments, wave a few heads of horse daisies, send out a few strains of odor from the blossoms of the white clover, and then die away fatigued with the effort. Turkey took out his Jew's harp, and played in soothing if not eloquent strains.

At our feet, a few yards from the mound, ran a babbling brook, which divided our farm from the next. Those of my readers whose ears are open to the music of nature must have observed how different are the songs sung by various brooks. Some are a mere tinkling; others, sweet as silver bells, with a tone besides which no bell ever had. Some sing in a careless, defiant tone.

This particular stream sang in a veiled voice, a contralto muffled in the hollows of overhanging banks, with a low, deep, musical gurgle in some of the stony eddies, in which a straw would float for days and nights till a flood came. The brook was deep for its size, and had a good deal to say in a solemn tone for such a small stream. We lay on the side of the hillock, as I said, and Turkey's Jew's harp mingled its sounds with those of the brook. After a while he laid it aside, and we were both silent for a time.

At length Turkey spoke.

"You've seen my mother, Ranald."

"Yes, Turkey."

"She's all I've got to look after."

"I haven't got any mother to look after, Turkey."

"No. You've got a father to look after you. I must do it, you know. My father wasn't so good to my mother. He used to get drunk sometimes, and then he was very rough with her. I must make it up to her as well as I can. She's not well off, Ranald."

"Isn't she, Turkey?"

"No. She works very hard at her spinning, and no one spins better than my mother. How could they? But she doesn't get paid much; you know, she'll be getting old by and by."

"Not tomorrow, Turkey."

"No, not tomorrow, nor the day after," said Turkey, looking up with some surprise to see what I meant by the remark.

But he then discovered that my eyes had led my thoughts astray. What he had been saying about his mother had got no further than into my ears. For on the opposite side of the stream, on the grass, like a shepherdess in an old picture, sat a young girl about my own age, in the midst of a crowded colony of daisies and white clover. She was knitting so that her needles went as fast as Kirsty's, and were nearly as invisible as the thing with the hooked teeth in it that looked so dangerous and ran itself out of sight upon Turkey's mother's spinning wheel. A little way from her was a fine cow, feeding with a long iron chain dragging after her. The girl was too far off for me to see her face very clearly. But something in her shape, her posture, and the hang of her head, I do not know what, had attracted me.

"There's Elsie Duff," said Turkey, noticing her a moment after I did, "with her granny's cow! I didn't know she was coming here today."

"Why is she feeding her on old James Joss's land?" I asked.

"Oh, they're very good to Elsie, you see. Nobody cares much about her grandmother, but Elsie's not her grandmother, and though the cow belongs to the old woman, for Elsie's sake, people here and there give her a bite of grass for it—usually a day's worth of feed. That cow's as plump as she needs to be, and has plenty of milk besides."

"I'll run down and tell her she may bring the cow into this field tomorrow," I said, getting up.

"I would if it were *mine*," said Turkey in a marked tone which stopped me.

"Oh, you mean I ought to ask my father."

"To be sure I do mean that," answered Turkey.

"Then I will ask him tonight," I returned.

How it happened I cannot now remember, but I know that after

all this I forgot to ask my father, and Granny Gregson's cow had no bite of grass off our land.

I soon grew quite strong again, and was before long back at my school labors. My father also had begun to take me in hand as well as my brother Tom to teach us what he could. And with arithmetic and Latin together, not to mention geography and history, I had quite enough to do, and quite as much also as was good for me.

CHAPTER
SIXTEEN

—

A NEW COMPANION

During this summer I made the acquaintance of a boy called Peter Mason. Peter was a clever boy, from whose merry eyes a sparkle was always ready to break. He seldom knew his lessons well, but when kept after hours for not knowing them, he always had learned the material before any of the rest of us had got halfway through it.

Among those around his own age and standing, he was the leader in the playground. He was even often invited to share in the amusements of the older boys. After school hours, he spent his time in all manner of pranks. In the hot summer weather he would go swimming twenty times a day, and was as much at home in the water as a duck. And that was how I came to be with him more than was good for me.

There was a certain small river not far from my father's house, which at a certain point was dammed back by large stones to turn part of it aside into a millrace. The mill stood a little way down, under a steep bank. It was almost surrounded by trees—willows at the water's edge, and birches and larches up the bank.

Above the dam was a fine spot for swimming, and the water was any depth you liked—from two to five or six feet. It was here that most of the boys of the village came to swim, and I with them.

I cannot recall the memory of those summer days without a gush of delight gurgling over my heart, just as the water used to gurgle over the stones of the dam. It was a quiet place, particularly on the side of my father's farm, which was sheltered by the same little wood that farther on surrounded the mill. The field which bordered the river was kept in natural grass, thick and short and fine. Here on the bank it grew well, although such grass was not at all common in that part of the country.

Oh, the summer days, with the hot sun drawing the smells from the feathery larch trees and the white-stemmed birches! I would get out of the water and lie in the warm soft grass, where now and then the tenderest little breeze would creep over my skin. When the sun had baked me more than was pleasant, I would rouse myself to my feet and run down to the border of the full-brimmed river, plunge again headlong into the quiet brown water, and dabble and swim till I was once more weary.

For innocent animal delight, I know of nothing to match those days—so warm, so pure-aired, so clean, so glad. I often think how God must love his little children to have invented for them such delights! For of course if he did not love the children and delight in their pleasure, he would not have invented the two and brought them together.

Yes, yes, I know what you would say: "But how many there are who have no such pleasures!"

I admit it sorrowfully. But you must remember that God is not done with them yet. And besides, there are more pleasures in the world than you or I know anything about. And if we had it *all* pleasure, I know I should not care so much about what is better, and I would rather be made good than have any other pleasures in the world. And so would you, though perhaps you do not know it yet.

One day a good many of us were at the water together. I felt rather important in my own eyes because I was swimming from my father's own land. The others had come to the bank on the other side, which had always been regarded as common to the village.

Suddenly, in the midst of them a man appeared who had recently rented the property. With him was a mean and villainous-looking dog. He ordered everyone off his land.

All the boys were undressed, and half of them were already swimming about in the river. At the man's threats, the rest were filled with terror and jumped in after them. All, that is, except one large boy, who showed no fear of the dog. Once in the water, several of the boys turned and began to mock the enemy, and from where I stood I told them all they would be welcome on the opposite bank.

All seemed well so far. But their clothes! They, alas, were still on the bank they had left!

The spirit of a host had come upon me, for I now regarded every one of them as my personal guests.

"You come ashore when you like," I said. "I will see what can be done about your clothes."

I knew that just below the dam lay a little boat built by the miller's son. It was clumsy enough, but to my eyes was nothing less than a marvel of engineering art. On the opposite side of the stream the big boy was still standing his ground bravely against the cur of a dog, which barked and growled at him, with its ugly head stretched out like a snake's. His owner, who was probably not so unkind as we thought him, stood enjoying the fun of it all.

I scrambled out of the water and ran for the boat. I jumped in and seized the oars, intending to row across and get the big boy to throw the clothes of the party into the boat. But I had never handled an oar in my life, and in the middle of the small river—how it happened I cannot tell—I found myself floundering in the water, and the boat overturned.

Now you might expect that since the water was dammed back that it would be shallow here where I was below the dam. But it was just the opposite. Had the bottom been hard, it would have been shallow. But as the bottom was soft and muddy, the rush of the water over the dam in the winter floods had here made a great hole. Besides this, there was another smaller dam a little way farther down. Right here where I had capsized, therefore, the depth was greater than anywhere on the river. Indeed, there were horrors afloat concerning its depth. I was a poor swimmer, for swimming is a natural gift and is not equally distributed to all.

I was struggling and floundering, half blind, with a sense of the water constantly getting up and stopping me and tossing me about no matter what I tried to do, when I felt myself laid hold of by the leg dragged under water, and a moment later landed safe on the bank. Almost the same moment I heard a plunge. I got up and, staggering and bewildered, saw a boy swimming after the boat, which had gone down with the slow current. He overtook it, scrambled into it in midstream, and at once took up the oars and put them to far better use than I had. When he had brought it back to the spot where I stood, I knew that Peter Mason was my deliverer.

I was quite recovered by this time from my slight attack of drowning. I got into the boat again, left the oars to Peter, and was rowed across and landed safely.

There was no further difficulty. I suppose the man was alarmed at the danger I had been in, and immediately recalled his dog. We bundled in the clothes, Peter rowed them across, Rory, the big boy, took to the water after the boat, and I plunged in again above the dam.

For the rest of that summer and part of the following winter, Peter was my hero, even to temporarily forgetting my friend Turkey. I took every opportunity to join Peter in his games—partly from gratitude, partly from admiration, but more than anything from the simple human attraction to the boy.

It was some time before he led me into any real mischief, but it came at last.

CHAPTER
SEVENTEEN
—

I GO DOWNHILL

I t came in the following winter.

As I told you, my father had now begun to teach me as well as Tom, but I confess I did not then value the privilege of being taught by one's own parent. I had become too fond of the society of Peter Mason. Always full of questionable frolic, the spirit of mischief gathered in him as the dark nights of the fall drew on. The sun and the wind and the green fields, and the flowing waters of summer kept him within bounds. But when the ice and the snow came, when the sky was gray with one solid cloud, when the wind was full of needle points of frost and the ground was hard as stone, when the evenings were dark, and the sun at noon shone low down and far away in the south, then the demon of mischief awoke in the heart of Peter Mason. And this winter, I am ashamed to say, it drew me also into the net.

Nothing very bad happened before the incident I am about to relate. However, there must have been a gradual sliding down toward it. Nobody does anything bad all at once. Wickedness needs a training period as well as more difficult trades.

It was in January, not long after the shortest day of the year, the sun setting about half past three o'clock. School was over and we were just coming out when Peter whispered to me, with one of his merriest twinkles in his eyes:

"Come across to town after dark, Ranald, and we'll have some fun."

I promised, and we arranged when and where to meet. It was Friday, and I had no Latin to prepare for Saturday; therefore my father did not want me for lessons. I remember feeling very jolly as I went home, and must have run ten times up and down the earthen wall, which parted the fields from the road by our house, watching for the sun to set.

After I had my dinner, I was so impatient to join Peter Mason that I could not rest, and from very idleness began to tease wee Davie. A great deal of that nasty teasing so common among boys comes from simply not having anything to do. At last poor Davie began to cry, and I, getting more and more wicked, went on teasing him, until finally he burst into a howl of wrath and misery. At that the Kelpie, who had some tenderness for him, burst into the room and boxed my ears soundly. I was in a fury of rage and revenge, and I am afraid if something had been nearby I might have thrown it at her.

I was still boiling with anger when I set off for the village to join Mason. I mention all this to show that I was in a bad state of mind, and thus prepared for the wickedness that followed. I repeat, a boy never gets into serious wrong all at once. He does not tumble from the top to the bottom of the cellar stairs. He goes down the steps himself till he comes to the broken one, and then he falls the rest of the way to the bottom all of a sudden when he stumbles on it.

When I reached the village, I found very few people about. The night was very cold, for there was a black frost. There had been a thaw the day before which had carried away most of the snow. But in the corners lay remnants of dirty heaps that had been swept up there. I was waiting near one of these, which happened to be at the spot where Peter had arranged to meet me, when a girl came out from a little shop nearby and walked quickly down the street. I yielded to the temptation arising in a mind which had grown dark with slimy things crawling in it. I kicked a hole in the frozen crust of the pile, scraped out a handful of dirty snow, kneaded it into a snowball, and set it flying after the girl.

It struck her on the back of the head. She gave a cry and ran away, with her hand to her forehead.

Brute that I was, I actually laughed. I think I must have been nearer the devil that night than I have ever been since. At least I hope so. For you see it was not with me as it might have been with worse-trained boys. I knew very well that I was doing wrong, and yet I refused to think about it. I felt bad inside. Peter might have done the same thing without being half as wicked as *I* was for doing it. He did not feel the wickedness of that kind of thing as I did. He would have laughed over it merrily. But the vile remains of my wrath with the Kelpie were still boiling away in my heart, and the horrid pleasure I found in annoying an innocent girl because the wicked Kelpie had made me angry could never come out of my mouth in a merry laugh like Mason's.

The fact is, I was more displeased with myself than with anybody else, though I would not admit it, and would not make myself stop and take the trouble to repent and do the right thing. If I had been able to say I was sorry to wee Davie once I saw that I was in the wrong, I think it may have kept me from all the other wicked things that followed. But I did not repent as I should have, and thus continued walking on down the cellar stairs to much worse badness yet.

In a little while Peter joined me. He laughed, of course, when I told him how the girl had run like a frightened hare. But in his eyes that was but small fun. He had bigger things in mind.

"Look here, Ranald," he said, holding out something like a piece of wood.

"What is it?" I asked.

"It's the stalk of a cabbage," he answered. "I've scooped out the inside and filled it with tow. We'll set fire to one end, and blow the smoke through the keyhole."

"Whose keyhole, Peter?"

"An old witch's that I know of. She'll be in such a rage! It'll be fun to hear her cursing and swearing. Come along. Here's a rope to tie her door with first."

I followed him, though I did have a few inward misgivings which I kept down as well as I could. I argued with myself, "I am not doing it. I am only going with Peter. What business is that of anybody's so long as I don't touch the thing myself?"

Only a few minutes more and I was helping Peter tie the rope to the latch handle of a poor little cottage, saying to myself, "This doesn't matter. This won't do her any harm. This isn't smoke. And after all, smoke won't hurt the nasty old thing. It'll only make her angry. It may even do her cough good: I daresay she's got a cough."

I knew everything I was saying to myself was false, and yet I acted on it. Was that not the very essence of wickedness itself?

One moment more and Peter was blowing through the hollow cabbage stalk in at the keyhole with all his might. Catching a breath of the foul stifling smoke himself, however, he began to cough violently and passed the wicked instrument to me. I put my mouth to it and blew as hard as I could. I believe now that there was some far more objectionable stuff mingled with the tow. In a few moments we heard the old woman begin to cough. Peter was peeping in at the window.

"She's getting up," he whispered. "Now we'll catch it, Ranald!"

Coughing as she came, I heard her shuffling steps approach the door, thinking to open it and let in fresh air. When she failed to open it because of Peter's rope, and saw where the smoke was coming from, she broke into a torrent of fierce and vengeful shouts, and calling of names. She did not curse and swear as Peter had led me to expect, although her language was certainly unrefined.

I laughed because I would not be unworthy of my companion, for Peter found great amusement in her anger. But in reality I was shocked at the storm I had been guilty of causing. I stopped blowing, aghast at what I had done. But Peter grabbed the tube from my hand and began the assault with fresh energy, whispering through the keyhole every now and then provoking and insulting words against the old woman, ridiculing her personal appearance and supposed ways of living. This threw her into new fits of rage and coughing. The war of words between the two increased, while she tugged at the door as she screamed, and he answered merrily. At length I lost all sense of right and wrong in the wicked game, and laughed loud and heartily.

All of a sudden the scolding and coughing stopped. A strange sound came, and again silence followed. Then came a shrill, suppressed scream, and we heard the voice of a girl crying.

"Grannie! Grannie!" she said. "What's the matter with you? Can't you speak to me, Grannie? They've smothered my grannie!"

Sobs and moans were all we heard now. Peter had become frightened at last, and was busy undoing the rope. Suddenly he flung the door wide open and fled, leaving me exposed to the full gaze of the girl.

To my horror, it was Elsie Duff!

She was just approaching the door, her eyes full of tears, and her sweet white face in agony. I stood unable to move or speak. She turned away without a word and began again to revive the old woman, who lay on the floor not two yards from the door. Finally guilt awoke fear and brought back my powers of movement. I fled at full speed, not to find Mason, but to leave everything behind me.

When I reached the manse, the starry blue night made it seem later than it actually was. Somehow I could not help thinking of the time when I came home after waking up in the barn. That too was a time of misery, but oh! how different from this! Then I myself had been cruelly treated. Now *I* had actually committed cruelty. Then I sought my father's embrace as the one refuge. Now I dreaded the very sight of my father, for I could not look him in the face. He was my father, but I was not his son.

I found myself giving a hurried glance at my life lately, and it revealed that I had been behaving very badly, and growing worse and worse. I became more and more miserable as I stood outside the house, and I did not know what to do. The cold at length drove me inside.

I usually sat with my father in his study during the winter evenings, but I didn't dare go near it now. I crept to the nursery, where I found a bright fire burning and Allister reading by the blaze while Davie lay in bed at the other side of the room. I sat down and warmed myself, but the warmth could not reach the lump of ice at my heart. I sat and stared at the fire. Allister was too absorbed in his book to pay any attention to me.

All at once I felt a pair of little arms about my neck, and Davie was trying to climb upon my knees. Instead of being comforting, however, I spoke very crossly, and sent him back to his bed whimpering. You see, I was at this point only miserable, but not repentant. I was eating the husks with the pigs, and did not like them. But I had not said, "I will arise and go to my father."

How I got through the rest of that evening I hardly know. I tried to read, but could not. I was rather fond of arithmetic, so I got my slate and tried to work a sum. But in a few moments I was sick of it. At family prayers I never lifted my head to look at my father. And when they were over, and I had said good night to him, I felt that I was sneaking out of the room. But I had some small sense of protection and safety once I was in bed beside little Davie. He was sound asleep and looked as innocent as little Samuel when the voice of God was going to call him. I put my arm around him, hugged him close to me, and began to cry, and the crying brought me sleep.

It had been a very long time since I had dreamed my old childish dream, but this night it returned. The old sunny-faced sun looked down upon me very solemnly. There was no smile on his big mouth, no twinkle about the corners of his little eyes. He looked at Mrs. Moon as much as to say, "What is to be done? The boy has been going the wrong way. Must we disown him?"

The moon neither shook her head nor moved her lips, but turned and stood with her back to her husband, looking very miserable. Not one of the star-children moved from its place. They shone sickly and small. In a little while they faded out altogether. Then the moon got paler and paler until she too vanished without ever turning her face to her husband. And at last the sun himself began to change. Only instead of getting pale, he drew in all his beams and shrank smaller and smaller, until he was no bigger than a candle flame.

Then I found that I was staring at a candle on the table, and that Tom was kneeling by the side of the other bed, saying his prayers.

CHAPTER
EIGHTEEN
—

THE TROUBLE GROWS

When I awoke in the morning, I tried to persuade myself that I had made a great deal too much of the whole business. I said in my mind that if it was not a particularly nice thing to do, it was at worst but a boy's trick. Only I would have nothing more to do with Peter Mason, who had betrayed me at the last moment.

I went to school as usual. It was the day we had to recite the Shorter Catechism. None failed at the assigned segments except Peter and me. We two were kept in alone and left in the schoolroom together.

I sat down as far from him as I could get. In half an hour he had learned the lesson, while I had not mastered the half of mine. Then he began, regardless of my pleas, to do all he could to prevent me learning it. He would pull the book away from me and talk in my ear, and annoyed me in twenty different ways. At last I began to cry, for Mason was a bigger and stronger boy than I, and there was nothing I could do to help myself against him.

After some time had passed, I lifted my head and thought I saw a shadow pass from the window. Although I could not positively say I saw it, I had a conviction it was Turkey, and my heart began to turn again toward him. I took some boldness from the thought and attempted my lesson once more. But that moment Peter was down upon me like a spider. He bothered me for a while longer, but then suddenly grew weary of the sport and stopped.

"You can stay if you like, Ran," he said. "But I've learned my catechism, and I don't see why I should stay in any longer."

As he spoke he drew a picklock from his pocket, and then proceeded to fiddle with the schoolroom door, succeeded in opening it, slipped out, and locked it behind him. Then he came to one of the windows and began making faces at me through it.

But vengeance was closer than he knew. The next instant a larger shadow darkened my page, and when I looked up, there was Turkey towering over Mason, with his hand on his collar and his whip lifted.

Mason received the threat as a joke, and laughed in Turkey's face. Yet sensing that Turkey looked dangerous, with a sudden wiggle, at which he was adept, he broke free. Trusting to his speed of foot, he turned his head and made a face at Turkey, then took to his heels. But before he could widen the space between them enough, Turkey's whip came down upon him.

With a howl of pain Peter doubled himself up, and Turkey fell upon him. Paying no attention to his yells and cries, Turkey pounded him severely. They were now too far away for me to distinguish words. I could hear that Turkey was lecturing him as well as punishing him. A little longer, and Peter crept past the window, looking miserable, his face bleared with crying, and his knuckles dug into his eyes.

And this was the boy I had chosen for my leader! He had been false to me, I said to myself, and the noble Turkey, seeing Peter's behavior through the window, had watched for an opportunity to give him the punishment he deserved. My heart was full of gratitude.

Turkey came near the window again, and then spoke to me. How dismayed I was to hear what he said.

"If you weren't your father's son, Ranald, and my own friend, I would do exactly the same to you."

An angry pride arose in me at the idea of Turkey, who used to call himself my horse, behaving to me in such a fashion. My evil ways had already half made a sneak of me.

"I'll tell my father!" I cried out.

"I only wish you would," he returned, "and then I should not be a tattletale if he asked me why and I told him all about it. You young scoundrel! You're no gentleman! To sneak about the streets and hit girls with snowballs! You should be scorned for what you did!"

"You must have been watching, then, Turkey, and you had no business to do that," I said, grabbing at even the stupidest defense.

"I was not watching. But if I had been, it would have been just as right as watching Hawkie. You ill-behaved creature!"

"It's a mean thing to do, Turkey," I persisted, seeking to stir up my own anger and blow up my pride all at once.

"I tell you I wasn't watching. I met Elsie Duff crying in the street because you had hit her with a dirty snowball. And then to go and smoke her and her poor grannie till the old woman fell down in a faint! You deserve a good beating yourself, I can tell you, Ranald. I'm ashamed of you."

He turned to go away. "Turkey, Turkey," I cried, "isn't the old woman better?"

"I don't know. I'm going to see," he answered.

"Come back and tell me, Turkey!" I shouted, as he disappeared from my field of vision.

"Indeed, I won't. I don't choose to keep company with such as you. But if I ever hear of you touching them again, you shall have more of me than you'll like, and you may tell your father so when you please."

I had indeed sunk low when Turkey, who had been such a friend, said he wanted to have nothing more to do with me. In a few minutes the schoolmaster returned, and finding me crying was touched with compassion. He sent me home at once. It was a good thing for me, for I would not have been able to answer a single question about the catechism. He thought Peter had crept out through one of the windows, and did not ask me about his disappearance.

The whole day was most miserable. I even hazarded one attempt at making friends with Mrs. Mitchell, but she repelled me so rudely that I did not try again. I could not bear the company of either Allister or Davie. I would have gone and told Kirsty, but I said to myself that Turkey must have already prejudiced her against me.

I went to bed that evening the moment prayers were over and slept a troubled sleep. I dreamed that Turkey had gone and told my father, and that he had turned me out of the house.

Chapter Nineteen

I TALK WITH
MY FATHER

I awoke early on Sunday morning. And a most dreary morning it was. I could not lie in bed. Although no one was up yet, I rose and got dressed. The house was as quiet as a tomb. I opened the front door and went out.

The rest of the world was no better. The day had hardly begun to dawn. The dark dead frost held it in chains of iron. The sky was dull and leaden, and cindery flakes of snow were thinly falling. Everywhere life looked utterly dreary and hopeless. What was there worth living for?

I went out on the road, and the ice in the ruts crackled under my feet like bones of dead things. I wandered away from the house, and the keen wind cut me to the bone. I had not even put on a coat before coming out. I turned into a field and stumbled along over its uneven surface of hard lumps. It was like walking on stones. The summer was gone and the winter was here, and my heart was colder and more miserable than any winter in the world.

I found myself at length at the little hill where Turkey and I had lain that lovely afternoon a year before. The stream below was quiet now with frost. The wind blew wearily but sharply across the bare field. There was no Elsie Duff with head drooping over her knitting, seated in the summer grass on the other side of a singing brook. Her head was aching on her pillow back in the village because I had struck her with that vile lump of snow. And instead of the smell of white clover, she was breathing the dregs of the hateful smoke with which I had filled the cottage.

I sat down, cold as it was, on the frozen hillock, and buried my face in my hands. Then my dream returned upon me. This was how I sat in my dream when my father had turned me out of doors. Oh, how dreadful it would be! I should just have to lie down and die!

I could not sit for long in the cold. Mechanically I rose and paced about. But I grew so wretched in my body from the cold that it made me forget for a while the trouble of my mind. Gradually I wandered home again.

The house was just stirring. I crept to the nursery, undressed, and lay down in bed beside little Davie, who cried out when my cold feet touched him. But I could not go to sleep again, although I lay there until everyone else had gone to the parlor. Finally I got up and joined them. I found them seated round a blazing fire waiting for my father.

He came in soon afterward, and we had our breakfast, and Davie gave his crumbs as usual to the robins and sparrows that came hopping on the windowsill. I imagined my father's eyes were often turned in my direction, but I could not lift mine up to see if it was true. I had never before known what true misery was!

Only Tom and I went to church that day: it was so cold. My father preached from the text, "Be sure your sin shall find you out."

I thought to myself that he had found out my sin and was preparing to punish me for it, and I was filled with terror as well as dismay. I could scarcely keep to my seat, I was so wretched and miserable. And when he said that a man's sin might find him out long before the punishment of it overtook him, and drew a picture of the misery of the wicked man who fled when no one was pursuing him, and was so miserable inside over what he had done that he trembled at the rustling sound of a leaf, then I was certain that he knew what I had done, or had seen through my face into my conscience.

When at last we went home, I kept waiting the whole of the day for the storm to break, expecting every moment to be called to his study. I did not enjoy a mouthful of my food, for I felt his eyes upon me, and they tortured me. I was like a shy creature of the woods whose hole has been stopped up: I had no place of refuge—nowhere to hide my head. I felt so naked! My very soul was naked.

After tea I slunk away to the nursery, and sat staring into the fire. Mrs. Mitchell came in several times and scolded me for sitting there instead of with Tom and the rest in the parlor. But I was too miserable to answer her. At length she brought Davie in and put him to bed. A few minutes later I heard my father coming down the stairs with Allister, who was chatting away to him. I wondered how he could.

My father came in with the big Bible under his arm, as was his custom on Sunday nights, drew a chair to the table, rang for candles to be brought, and with the rest of us seated and Davie in bed, he began to find a place from which to read to us.

To make my conviction all the stronger that he knew everything, he began and read through the parable of the Prodigal Son without so much as a remark. When he came to the father's delight at having him back, the robe, the shoes, and the ring, I could not repress my tears.

If I could only go back, I thought, *and set it all right! but then I've never gone away.*

It was a foolish thought, instantly followed by a longing impulse to tell my father all about it. I had been waiting all this time for my sin to find me out. Why should I not frustrate my sin, and find my father first?

As soon as he was done reading and before he had opened his mouth to make any remark, I crept round the table to his side and whispered in his ear.

"Papa, I want to speak to you."

"Very well, Ranald," he said, more solemnly, I thought, than usual. "Come up to my study."

He rose and led the way. I followed. A whimper of disappointment came from Davie's bed. My father went and kissed him and said he would be back soon. Then Davie nestled down in his bed satisfied.

When we reached the study, he closed the door, sat down by the fire, and drew me toward him.

I burst out crying, and could not speak for sobs. He encouraged me most kindly.

"Have you been doing anything wrong, my boy?" he said.

"Yes, Papa, very wrong," I sobbed. "I hate myself for it."

"I am glad to hear it, my dear," he returned. "There is some hope for you then."

"Oh, I don't know," I answered. "Even Turkey despises me."

101

"That is very serious," said my father. "Turkey's a fine fellow. I should not like him to despise me. But tell me all about it."

It was with great difficulty that I began, but with the help of questioning me, my father at length understood the whole matter. He paused for a while deep in thought. Then he rose.

"It's a serious affair, my boy," he said. "But now that you have told me, I shall be able to help you."

"But you knew about it before, didn't you, Papa? Surely you did."

"Not a word of it, Ranald. You thought so because your sin had found you out. I must go and see how the poor woman is. I don't want to reproach you at all now that you are sorry. But I should like you just to think that you have been helping to make that poor old woman wicked. She is naturally of a sour disposition, and you have made it sourer still, and no doubt have made her hate everybody more than she was already inclined to do. You have been working against God right here in my parish."

I burst into fresh tears. It was too dreadful! "What *am* I to do?" I cried.

"You must go and beg Mrs. Gregson's pardon, and tell her that you are both sorry and ashamed."

"Yes, Papa. Will you let me go with you?"

"It's too late today to find her still up, I'm afraid. But we can go and see. We've done a wrong, a very grievous wrong, my boy, and I cannot rest till I at least know the consequences of it."

He put on his long overcoat and muffler hastily, and having seen that I too was properly wrapped up, he opened the door and we stepped out into the wintry evening cold. But then remembering the promise he had made to Davie, he turned and went down to the nursery to speak to him again while I waited for him on the doorsteps. It would have been quite dark but for the stars, and there was no snow to give back any of their shine. The earth swallowed all their rays and was no brighter for it. But oh, what a change to me from the frightful morning! When my father returned, I put my hand in his almost as fearlessly as Allister or wee Davie might have done, and we walked away toward the village together.

"Papa," I said, "why did you say *we* have done a wrong? You did not do it."

"My dear boy," he replied, "persons who are so near each other as we are must not only bear the consequences together of any wrong done by one of them, but must, in a sense, even bear each other's sins. If I do something wrong, you must suffer. If you sin, you being my own boy, I must suffer."

"Why should you suffer for what I have done?"

"Because you are my son. I am responsible for you. I am accountable not only for myself, but for you as well. And this is not all. It lies upon both of us to do what we can to get rid of the wrong done, and thus we have to bear each other's sin. I am accountable to make amends as far as I can, and also to do what I can to get you to be sorry and make amends as far as you can."

"But, Papa, isn't that hard?" I asked.

"Do you think I should like to leave you to get out of your sin as best you could, or sink deeper and deeper into it? Do you not know I would do *all* I could to help free you from it? Should I grudge anything to take the weight of the sin, or the wrong to others, off you? Do you think I should want not to be troubled about it? Or if *I* were to do anything wrong, would you think it hard on *you* that had to help *me* to be good, and set things right?"

"Oh no, Papa."

"Even if people looked down on you because of me, would you say it was hard on you? Wouldn't you gladly help me? Wouldn't you say to yourself, 'I am glad to bear anything for my father! I'll share it with him'?"

"Yes, indeed, Papa!"

"Of course you would. Just as I would bear anything for you."

"I would rather share with you than be alone, whatever it was."

"Then you see, my boy, how kind God is in tying us up in one bundle together that way. That's what it means to bear one another's burdens. We are bound together in one great fellowship of brotherhood and sisterhood, which is all the greater in a family. It is a grand and beautiful thing that the fathers should suffer for their children, and the children for their fathers. I don't see it as a hard thing at all, but the most natural thing in the world."

"It doesn't sound hard to hear you talk of it, Papa."

"Hard perhaps, Ranald, my boy. But the love underneath it makes the consequences able to be borne bravely. Come along. We must step out, or I fear we shall not be able to make our apology tonight. When we've gotten over this, Ranald, we must be a good deal more careful what company we keep."

"Oh, Papa," I said, "if only Turkey would forgive me!"

"There's no fear of that. Turkey is sure to forgive you when you've done what you can to make amends. He's a fine fellow, Turkey. I have a high opinion of Turkey—as you call him."

"If he would, Papa, I would not wish for any other company than his."

"A boy needs various kinds of friends, Ranald. But I fear you have been neglecting Turkey. You owe him much."

"Yes, indeed, I do, Papa," I answered. "And I have been neglecting him. If I had kept with Turkey, I should never have got into such a dreadful scrape as this."

"That is too light a word to use for it, my boy. Don't call wickedness a mere scrape. For wickedness it certainly was, though I am only too willing to believe you had no true idea at the time just *how* wicked it really was."

"I won't ever do such a thing again, Papa. But I am so relieved already."

"Perhaps poor old Mrs. Gregson is not relieved though. You ought not to forget her."

Thus talking, we hurried on until we arrived at the cottage. A dim light was visible through the window. My father knocked, and Elsie Duff opened the door.

FORGIVENESS

When we entered, there sat the old woman on the farther side of the hearth, rocking herself to and fro.

I hardly dared look up.

Elsie's face was composed and sweet. She gave me a shy tremulous smile, which went to my heart and humbled me dreadfully. My father took the stool on which Elsie had been sitting. When he had lowered himself upon it, his face was nearly on a level with that of the old woman, who took no notice of him, but kept rocking herself to and fro and moaning.

He laid his hand on hers, which, old and withered and not very clean, lay on her knee.

"How are you tonight, Mrs. Gregson?" he asked.

"I'm an ill-used woman," she replied with a groan, behaving as if it were my father who had mistreated her, and whose duty it was to make an apology for it.

"I am aware of what you mean, Mrs. Gregson. That is what brought me to ask about you. I hope you are not seriously the worse for it."

"I'm an ill-used woman," she repeated. "Every man's hand is against me."

"Well, I hardly think that," said my father in a cheerful tone.

105

"*My* hand's not against you now."

"If you bring up your sons to mock at the poor, Mr. Bannerman," she said, "and find their amusement in driving the old and sick to death's door, you can't say your hand's not against a poor lone woman like me."

"But I don't bring up my sons to do so. If I did I shouldn't be here now. I am willing to bear my part of the blame, Mrs. Gregson. And for that part, I humbly beg your forgiveness. But to say I bring my sons up to that kind of wickedness is to lay on me a good deal more than my share. Come here, Ranald."

I obeyed, with bowed head and shame-stricken heart. I now saw what a tremendous wrong I had done my father as well. He was attempting to live as God's man in the parish, and to tell people of God's love and care for them, and I had done *this* to him! I could hardly bear the thought of it! And although few people would be so unjust to him as this old woman, many would yet blame him, the best man in the world, for the wrongs of his children.

When I stood by my father's side, the old woman just lifted her head once to cast on me a scowling look, and then went on again rocking herself.

"Now, my boy," said my father, "tell Mrs. Gregson why you have come here tonight."

I had to use a dreadful effort to make myself speak. It was like resisting a dumb spirit and forcing the words from my lips. But I did not hesitate a moment. In fact, I dared not hesitate, for I felt that hesitation would be defeat.

"I came, Papa—" I began.

"No, no, my man," interrupted my father; "you must speak to Mrs. Gregson, not to me."

Thereupon I had to make a brand-new effort, more dreadful yet. It was all I could do to summon the courage to look up at the old woman's face.

To this day, whenever I see a child who will not say the words required of him, I feel again just as I felt then, and think how difficult it is for him to do what he is told. But oh, how I wish he would do it that he might be a conqueror! For I know that if he will not make the effort, it will grow more and more difficult for him to make any effort. I cannot be too thankful that my father did not allow me to shy away from facing the consequences of what I had done squarely—so squarely that I had to look the very object of my sin in the face! And how thankful I am that I was able to overcome the difficulty of the effort before me at that moment.

"I came, Mrs. Gregson," I faltered, "to tell you that I am very sorry I behaved so badly to you."

"Yes, indeed," she returned, following it with a bit of a *humpf!* My eyes sought the floor.

"How would you like anyone to come and do such in your nice big house?" she added, still in a grumpy voice. "But a poor lonely widow woman like me is nothing to be thought of. Oh no! Not at all!"

"I am ashamed of myself," I said, almost forcing my confession upon her.

"So you ought to be all the days of your life. You deserve to be drummed out of the town for the minister's son that you are! Hoo!"

"I'll never do it again, Mrs. Gregson."

"You'd better not, or you shall hear of it, if there's a sheriff in the county. To insult honest people that way!"

I drew back, more conscious than ever of the wrong I had done in rousing such unforgiving fierceness in the heart of a woman. My father spoke up now.

"Shall I tell you, Mrs. Gregson," he said kindly, "what made the boy sorry, and made him willing to come and tell you all about it?"

"Oh, I've got friends after all. The young prodigal!"

"You are getting pretty near the answer to my question, Mrs. Gregson," said my father, "but you haven't quite touched it yet."

"Humpf!" she muttered.

"It was a friend of yours who spoke to my boy and made him very unhappy about what he had done, telling him over and over again what a shameful thing it was, and how wicked he had been."

"I've got friends, I tell you."

"Do you know what friend it was?"

"Perhaps I do, perhaps I don't. I can guess," she said, still with a sour tone.

"I fear you don't guess quite correctly. It was the best friend you ever had or ever will have."

This time her *humpf* was said almost to herself.

"It was God himself talking in my poor boy's heart," my father went on, looking upon her with love in his eyes. "Ranald would not heed what God said all day, but in the evening we were reading how the Prodigal Son went back to his father, and how the father forgave him. And poor Ranald couldn't stand it any longer, and came and told me all about it."

"It wasn't you he had to go to. It wasn't you he smoked to death—was it now? It was easy enough for him to go to you!"

"Not so easy, perhaps. But he has come to you now."

"Come when you made him come!"

"I didn't make him. He came gladly. He saw it was all he could do to make up for the wrong he had done."

"A poor amends!" I heard her grumble. But my father took no notice.

"And you know, Mrs. Gregson," he went on, "when the Prodigal Son did go back to his father, his father forgave him at once."

"Easy enough! He was his father, and fathers always side with their sons."

I saw my father thinking for a moment.

"Yes, that is true," he said. "And what he does himself, he always wants his sons and daughters to do. So he tells us that if we don't forgive one another, he will not forgive us. And as we all want to be forgiven, we had better mind what we're told."

"Humpf" came softly from the chair, which had nearly ceased in its rocking.

"And if you don't forgive this boy, who has done you a great wrong but is sorry for it, God will not forgive you—and that's a serious affair."

"He's never begged my pardon yet," said the old woman, whose dignity required the utter humiliation of the offender.

"I beg your pardon, Mrs. Gregson," I said. "I shall never be rude to you again. Please forgive me."

"Very well," she answered, a little mollified at last. "Keep your promise, and we shall say no more about it. It's for your father's sake, mind, that I forgive you."

I saw a smile trembling about my father's lips, but he suppressed it.

"Won't you shake hands with him, Mrs. Gregson?" he asked.

She held out a poor shriveled hand, which I took very gladly. It felt so strange in mine that I was frightened at it. It was like something half dead.

But at the same moment, from behind me another hand, a rough little hand, but warm and firm and all alive, slipped into my left hand. I knew it was Elsie Duff's, and the thought of how I had behaved to her rushed in upon me with a cold misery of shame.

I would have knelt at her feet, but I could not tell her of my sorrow in front of witnesses. Therefore I kept hold of her hand and led her by it to the other end of the cottage, for there was a friendly gloom, the only light in the place coming from the glow—not the flame—of a fire of peat and bark. She came with me readily, whispering before I had time to open my mouth.

"I'm sorry Grannie's so hard to make it up with."

"I deserve it," I said. "Elsie, I was a brute. I could knock my head on the wall. Please forgive me."

"It's not me," she answered. "You didn't hurt me. I didn't mind it."

"Oh, Elsie! I struck you with that horrid snowball."

"It was only on the back of my neck. It didn't hurt me much. It only frightened me."

"I didn't know it was you. If I had known, I'm sure I wouldn't have done it. But it was wicked and contemptible to anyone, to any girl."

I broke down again, half from shame, half from the happiness of having cast my sin away from me by confessing it. Elsie held my hand now.

"Never mind, never mind," she said. "It's over now, and you won't do it again."

"I would rather be hanged," I sobbed.

That moment a pair of strong hands caught hold of mine, and the next instant I found myself hoisted on somebody's back by a succession of heaves and pitches, which did not stop until I was firmly seated. Then a voice spoke.

"I'm his horse again, Elsie, and I'll carry him home this very night."

Elsie gave a pleased little laugh, and Turkey bore me away to the fireside, where my father was talking away in a low tone to the old woman. I believe he had now turned the tables upon her, and was trying to convince her of her unkind and grumbling ways. But he did not let us hear a word of the reproof.

"Eh, Turkey, my lad! Is that you?" said my father. "I didn't know you were there."

I had never before heard my father address him as Turkey.

"What are you doing with that great boy on your back?" he continued.

"I'm going to carry him home, sir."

"Nonsense! He can walk well enough."

Half ashamed of being the center of such attention, I began to struggle to get down. But Turkey held me tight.

"But you see, sir," said Turkey, "we're friends now. *He's* done what he could, and *I* want to do what I can."

"Very well," returned my father, rising. "Come along then; it's time we were going."

When he said good night to her, the old woman actually rose and held out her hand to both of us.

"Good night, Grannie," said Turkey. "Good night, Elsie." And away we went. Never a conqueror on his triumphal entry was happier than I as through the starry night I rode home on Turkey's back. The very stars seemed to be rejoicing over my head. When I think of it now, the words always come with it, "There is joy in the presence of the angels of God over one sinner that repents," and I cannot but believe they rejoiced at that moment. For if ever I repented in my life, I repented then.

When at length I was down in bed beside Davie, it seemed as if there could be nobody in the world so blessed as I. I had been forgiven!

When I awoke in the morning, it was like being born into a new world. Before getting up I had a rare game with Davie, whose shrieks of laughter at length brought Mrs. Mitchell with an angry face. But I found myself feeling kindly even toward her.

The weather was much the same, but its dreariness had vanished. There was a glowing spot in my heart that drove out the cold, and glorified the black frost that bound the earth.

When I went out before breakfast and saw the red face of the

sun looking through the mist like a bright copper kettle, he seemed to know all about it, and to be friends with me as he had never been before. And I was quite as well satisfied as if the sun of my dream had given me a friendly nod of forgiveness.

CHAPTER
Twenty-one

—

I Have a Fall

E lsie Duff's father was a farm laborer, with a large family. He
was what is called a cotter in Scotland, which means that he
worked for yearly wages on a large farm, and had a little bit of land
to cultivate for his own use. His wife's mother was Grannie Gregson.

Now Grannie was so old that she needed someone to look after
her. But she had a cottage of her own in the village, and would not
go and live with her daughter. Indeed, they were not anxious to
have her, for she was not by any means a pleasant person. So there
was no way to help it—Elsie had to go and be her companion.

It was a great trial to her at first, for her home was a happy one,
and her mother was very unlike Elsie's grandmother. And besides,
she preferred the open fields to the streets of the village. She did
not grumble, however, for what is the good of grumbling where
duty is plain, or even when a thing cannot be helped? She found
it very lonely though, especially when her grannie was in one of
her gloomy or grumpy moods. Then she would not answer a single
question but leave the poor girl to do what she thought best, and
complain of it afterward.

This was partly the reason her parents, toward the close of
spring, sent a little brother—who was too delicate to be of much

use on the farm at home—to spend some months with his grannie and go to school. The original intention had been that Elsie herself should go to school, but what with the cow and the grandmother together she had not been able to begin. Of course, Grannie grumbled at the proposed change. But as Turkey—my informant on these matters—explained, she was afraid that if she objected too much they would take Elsie away and send a younger sister in her place. So little Jamie Duff came to join Elsie at Grannie's, and began coming to the school.

He was a poor little white-haired, red-eyed boy, who found himself very much out of his element there. Some of the bigger boys imagined it good fun to tease him. But on the whole he was rather a favorite, for he looked so pitiful, and took everything so patiently.

For my part, I was delighted at the chance of showing Elsie Duff some kindness through her brother. The girl's sweetness clung to me, and not only made it impossible for me to be rude to any girl, but kept me awake for any opportunity to do something for her sake.

One day before the master arrived, I perceived that Jamie was shivering with cold. I made way for him where I was standing by the fire, and then found that he had next to nothing on his little body, and that the soles of his shoes were hanging half off. This in the month of March in the north of Scotland was bad enough, even if he had not had a cough.

I told my father when I went home, and he sent me to tell Mrs. Mitchell to find some old garments of Allister's for him. She declared there were none. When I told Turkey this he looked very grave, but said nothing. When I told my father, he told me to take the boy to the tailor and shoemaker and get some warm and strong clothes and shoes made for him.

I was proud enough of the assignment. And if I did act a little too much like the grand benefactor, I am still bearing the shame of it still. Of how many people shall I not have to beg the precious forgiveness when I meet them in the other world! Perhaps I shall say this for myself, that I never thought of demanding any service from the little fellow in return for mine. I was not so bad as that. And I was true in heart to him in spite of my pride, for I had a real affection for him. I had not spoken to his sister since the Sunday night of my confession in the cottage.

One Saturday afternoon, as we were having a game something like Hare and Hounds, I was running very hard through the village when my foot landed on a loose stone, and I had a violent fall.

When I got up, I saw Jamie Duff standing by my side with a look of utter consternation. I discovered afterward that he was in the habit of following me about. Finding blood on my face and thinking when I came to myself that I was very near the house where Turkey's mother lived, I crawled to my feet and hobbled to it, and up the stairs to her garret. Jamie followed me in silence.

I found her busy as usual at her spinning wheel, and Elsie Duff stood talking to her, as if she had just run in for a moment and could not even take the time to sit down.

The moment she saw the state I was in, Elsie gave a little cry. Turkey's mother got up and made me take her chair, while she hurried to get some water. I grew faint and lost consciousness. When I came to myself I was leaning against Elsie, whose face was as white as a sheet with worry. I drank a little water and soon began to revive.

When Turkey's mother had bandaged up my head with some rags, I rose to go home. But she persuaded me to lie down a while. I was perfectly willing to comply. What a sense of blissful repose came over me, weary with running and feeling faint from the fall and loss of blood, when I stretched myself out on the bed. Its patchwork blanket, let me say for Turkey's mother, was as clean as any down quilt in any room of the rich.

I remember so vividly how a single ray of sunlight fell on the floor from the little window in the roof so that it hit just on the foot that kept turning the spinning wheel. Its hum sounded in my sleepy ears as Turkey's mother sent it again into motion. I gazed at the sloping ray of light, in which the ceaseless rotation of the swift wheel kept the motes of dust dancing most busily. At length, to my half-closed eyes, the beam became a huge Jacob's ladder, crowded with an innumerable company of ascending and descending angels, and I thought it must be the same ladder I used to see in my dream.

The drowsy delight which follows a light-headed faint pos-

sessed me. And the little garret with the slanting roof, and its sloping sunray, and the whir of the wheel, and the form of the patient
woman that was spinning, all began to gather about them the hues
of Paradise to my slowly fading senses. And then I heard a voice
that sounded miles away, and yet close to my ear:

"Elsie, sing a little song, will you?"

I heard no reply. A pause followed, and then a voice, clear and
melodious as a brook, began to sing. And before it stopped, I was
indeed in a kind of paradise.

CHAPTER

TWENTY-TWO

SONG AND DREAMS

I promised myself when I began that I would not offend fastidious ears with a single syllable of the rough tongue of my native Scotch, but would tell my story in English. Shall I be breaking that promise if I give the song just as Elsie sang it? True, it is not part of the story exactly, but it is in it. And if you would like the song, you will have to have it in Scotch or not at all. I am not going to spoil it by turning it out of its own natural clothes into finer garments to which it was not born—I mean by translating the Scotch into English.

The best way will be this: I will give you the song as something extra—call it a footnote slipped into the middle of the page. Nobody needs read a word of it to understand the story.

SONG

Oh! the bonny, bonny dell, whaur the yorlin[1] sings,
Wi' a clip o' the sunshine atween his wings;
Whaur the birks[2] are a' straikit wi' fair munelicht,
And the broom hings its lamps by day and by nicht;
Whaur the burnie comes trottin' ower shingle and stane,

---
[1]The yellow hammer
[2]Birch trees

116

Liltin'[3] bonny havers[4] til 'tsel alane;
And the sliddery[5] troot wi'ae soop o' its tail,
Is awa' 'neath the green weed's swingin' veil!
Oh! the bonny, bonny dell, whaur I sang as I saw
The yorlin, the broom, an' the burnie, an' a'!

Oh! the bonny, bonny dell, whaur the primroses wonn
Luikin' oot o' their leaves like wee sons o' the sun;
Whaur the wild roses hing like flickers o' flame,
And fa' at the touch wi' a dainty shame;
Whaur the bee swings ower the white clovery sod,
And the butterfly flits like a stray thoucht o' God;
Whaur, like arrow shot frae life's unseen bow,
The dragon-fly burns the sunlicht throu'!
Oh! the bonny, bonny dell, whaur I sang to see
The rose and the primrose, the draigon and bee!

Oh! the bonny, bonny dell, whaur the mune luiks doon
As gin she war hearin' a soundless tune,
Whan the flowers an' the birds are a' asleep,
And the verra burnie gangs creepy-creep;
Whaur the corn-craik craiks in the lang rye
And the nicht is the safter for his rouch cry;
Whaur the wind wad fain lie doon on the slope,
And the verra darkness owerflows wi' hope!
Oh! the bonny, bonny dell, whaur, silent, I felt
The mune an' the darkness baith into me melt.

Oh! the bonny, bonny dell, whaur the sun luiks in,
Sayin', Here awa', there awa', haud awa', sin!
Wi' the licht o' God in his flashin' ee,
Saying, Darkness and sorrow a' work for me!
Whaur the lark springs up on his ain sang borne,
Wi' bird-shout and jubilee hailin' the morn;
For his hert is fu' o' the hert o' the licht,
An', come darkness or winter, a' maun be richt!
Oh! the bonny, bonny dell, whaur the sun luikit in,
Sayin', Here awa', there awa', haud awa', sin.

Oh! the bonny, bonny dell, whaur I used to lie

[3]Singing
[4]Nonsense
[5]Slippery

117

Wi' Jeanie aside me, sae sweet and sae shy!
Whaur the wee white gowan wi' reid tips,
Was as white as her cheek and as reid as her lips.
Oh, her ee had a licht cam frae far 'yont the sun,
And her tears cam frae deeper than salt seas run!
O' the sunlicht and munelicht she was the queen,
For baith war but middlin' withoot my Jean.
Oh! the bonny, bonny dell, whaur I used to lie
Wi' Jeanie aside me, sae sweet and sae shy!

Oh! the bonny, bonny dell, whaur the kirkyard lies,
A' day and a' nicht, luikin' up to the skies;
Whaur the sheep wauk up i' the summer nicht,
Tak a bite, and lie doon, and await the licht;
Whaur the psalms roll ower the grassy heaps,
And the wind comes and moans, and the rain comes and weeps!
But Jeanie, my Jeanie—she's no lyin' there,
For she's up and awa' up the angels' stair.
Oh! the bonny, bonny dell, whaur the kirkyard lies,
And the stars luik doon, and the nicht-wind sighs!

Elsie's voice went through every corner of my brain. There was singing in all its rooms. I could not hear the words of the song well enough to understand them fully. But Turkey gave me a copy of them afterward. They were the schoolmaster's work. All that winter Turkey had been going to the evening school, and the master had been greatly pleased with him, and had done his best to get him on in various ways. A friendship sprang up between them, and one night he showed Turkey these verses. Where the tune came from I do not know. Elsie's brain was full of tunes. I repeated them to my father once, and he was greatly pleased with them.

On this first acquaintance, however, they put me to sleep, and little Jamie Duff was sent over to tell my father what had happened. Jamie gave the message to Mrs. Mitchell. And she, full of her own importance, had to set out immediately to see how much was the matter—without, of course, informing my father about the incident.

I was dreaming an unutterably delicious dream. It was a summer evening. The sun was of a tremendous size, and a splendid rose color. He was resting with his lower edge on the horizon, and dared go no farther because all the flowers would sing instead of giving out their proper scents; and if he left them, he feared utter anarchy in his kingdom before he got back in the morning.

I woke and saw the ugly face of Mrs. Mitchell bending over me. She was pushing me and calling to wake me up. The moment I saw her I shut my eyes tight, turned away, and pretended to be fast asleep again in the hope that she would go away and leave me with my friends.

"Let him have his sleep out, Mrs. Mitchell," said Turkey's mother.

"You've let him sleep too long already," she returned ungraciously. "He'll do all he can, waking or sleeping, to make himself troublesome. He'll never come to anything, that Ranald. It's a mercy his mother is under the ground, for he would have broken her heart."

I was quite awake by this time, but I was not in the least inclined to acknowledge it to Mrs. Mitchell.

"You're wrong there, Mrs. Mitchell," said Elsie Duff. And you must remember it required a good deal of courage to stand up against a woman so much older than herself, and occupying the important position of housekeeper to the minister. "Ranald is a good boy. I'm sure he is."

"How dare you say so, when he served your poor old grandmother such a wicked trick? Don't you speak to me again."

"No, don't, Elsie," said another voice, accompanied by a creaking of the door and a heavy step. "Don't speak to her, Elsie, or you'll have the worst of it. Leave her to me.—If Ranald did what you say, Mrs. Mitchell," Turkey went on, "and I don't deny it, he was at least very sorry for it afterward, and begged Grannie's forgiveness. And that's a sort of thing *you* never did in your life."

"I have never had occasion to, Turkey, so you hold your tongue."

"Don't you call me *Turkey*. I won't stand for it. I was christened as well as you."

"And what are *you* to speak to me like that? Go home to your cows. I daresay they're standing supperless in their stalls while you're gadding about. I'll call you *Turkey* as long as I please."

"Very well, Kelpie—that's the name you're known by, though perhaps no one has been polite enough to use it to your face, for you're a great woman, no doubt—I give you warning that I know you. When you're found out, don't say I didn't give you a chance beforehand."

"You impudent beggar!" cried Mrs. Mitchell in a rage. "You're all one pack," she added, looking round on the others. "Get up, Ranald, and come home with me directly. What are you lying there pretending for?"

As she spoke she approached the bed. But Turkey was too quick for her and got in front of it. As he had by this time become a great strong lad, she dared not lay hands on him. So she turned in a rage and stalked out of the room.

"Mr. Bannerman shall hear of this," she said.

"Then it shall be both sides of it, Mrs. Mitchell," I cried from the bed. But she vanished, giving me no reply.

Once more Turkey got me on his back and carried me home. I told my father the whole occurrence. He examined the cut and dressed it with medicine for me, saying he would go and thank Turkey's mother at once. I confess I thought more of Elsie Duff and her wonderful singing, which had put me to sleep and given me the strange lovely dream from which the rough hands and harsh voice of the Kelpie had waked me too soon.

After this, although I never dared go near her grandmother's house alone, I yet had many a peep of Elsie. Sometimes I went with Turkey to his mother's in an evening, to which my father had no objection, and somehow or other Elsie was sure to be there. Sometimes she would sing, or sometimes I would read to them out of Milton, and though there was much we could not understand in it, I am certain we all grew by it regardless. It is not necessary that the intellect can understand completely before the heart and soul derive nourishment. As well say that a bee can get nothing out of a flower because she does not understand botany. The very music of the stately words of a grand poem is enough to generate a higher mood, to make one feel the air of higher regions. The best influences which bear upon us are of this vague sort—powerful upon the heart and conscience, although undefined to the intellect.

But I find that I have been forgetting that those for whom I write are young—too young to understand all this.

Let it remain, however, for those older persons who at an odd moment, while waiting for dinner or before going to bed, may take up a little one's book and turn over a few of its leaves. Some such readers, in virtue of their hearts being young and old both at once, discern more in the children's books than the children themselves.

—

Chapter Twenty-three

THE BEES' NEST

I t was noon on a delicious Saturday in the height of summer.
We poured out of school with the gladness of a holiday in
our hearts. I sauntered home full of the summer sun, and the summer wind, and the summer scents which filled the air. I do not
know how often I sat down in perfect bliss upon the earthen walls
that divided the fields from the roads, and basked in the heat.

These walls were covered with grass and moss. The odor of a
certain yellow feathery flower, which grew on them rather plenti-
fully, used to give me special delight. Great bumblebees haunted
the walls, and were poking about in them constantly. Butterflies
also found them pleasant places, and I delighted in butterflies,
though I seldom succeeded in catching one. I do not remember that
I ever killed one. Heart and conscience were both against that.

I had got the loan of Mrs. Trimmer's story about a family of
robins, and was every now and then reading a page of it with
unspeakable delight. We had very few books for children in those
days and in that far out-of-the-way place, and those we did get
were all the more dearly prized.

It was almost dinnertime before I reached home. Somehow in
this grand weather, welcome as dinner always was, it did not pos-
sess the same amount of interest as in the cold bitter winter. On

this day I almost hurried over mine to get out again into the broad sunlight. Oh, how stately the hollyhocks towered on the borders of the shrubbery! Here and there damask roses, dark almost to blackness, and with a soft velvety surface, enriched the sunny air with their color and their scent. I never see these roses now. And the little bushes of polyanthus gemmed the dark earth between with their varied hues. We did not know anything about flowers except the delight they gave us. And I daresay I am putting some together which would not be blooming at the same time, but that is how the picture comes back to my memory.

I was leaning in utter idleness over the gate that separated the little lawn and its surroundings from the road when a troop of children passed with little baskets and tin pails in their hands. Among them was Jamie Duff. It was not in the least necessary to ask him where he was going.

Not very far from our house, about a mile or so, rose a certain hill famed in the country round for its great store of bilberries. It was the same hill to which Turkey and I had fled for refuge from the bull. It was called Ba' Hill, and a tradition lingered in the neighborhood that many years ago there had been a battle there, and that after the battle the conquerors played at football with the heads of those they had slain. And hence came the name of the hill. But who fought or which conqueror, there was not a shadow of a record. Scotland had been a wild country, and conflicting clans had often made fierce and wild work in it.

In summer the hill was of course the haunt of children gathering its bilberries. Jamie shyly suggested that I might join them. But they were all too much younger than I. And besides, I felt drawn to seek Turkey in the field with the cattle—that is, when I should get quite tired of doing nothing. So the little troop streamed on, and I remained leaning over the gate.

I suppose I had sunk into a dreamy state, for I was suddenly startled by a sound beside me. Looking about I saw an old woman, bent nearly double within an old gray cloak, in spite of the heat. She leaned on a stick, and carried a bag like a pillowcase in her hand. It was one of the poor people of the village, going on her rounds for her weekly hand-out of oatmeal from those kind enough to give her some.

123

I knew her very well by sight and by name. She was old Eppie, and a kindly greeting passed between us. There was no shame in honest poverty in those days, and it was no burden to those who helped such people as Eppie. Everyone knew everyone else, and kindly feelings existed on both sides. If I understand anything of human nature now, it comes partly of having known and respected the poor of my father's parish.

She passed in at the gate and went as usual to the kitchen door, while I stood drowsily looking at the green expanse of growing crops in the valley in front of me. The day had grown as sleepy as I was. There were no noises except the hum of the unseen insects, and the distant rush of the water over the dams at our swimming hole. In a few minutes the old woman approached me again. She was an honest and worthy soul, and very polite in her manners. Therefore, I was surprised to hear her muttering to herself.

Turning around, I saw that she was very angry. She stopped her muttering when she saw me watching her, and walked on in silence. Something had made her angry, and instinctively I put my hand in my pocket and pulled out a halfpenny my father had given me that morning—very few of which came my way. As she was about to pass by me, I offered it to her.

She took it with a half-ashamed glance, an attempt at a courtsy, and a murmured blessing. Then for a moment she looked as if she were about to say something. But she changed her mind, and only added another grateful word, and hobbled away.

I pondered the situation feebly for a moment and came to the conclusion that the Kelpie had been rude to her, and then promptly forgot about it and fell to dreaming again. Growing tired at length of doing nothing, I roused myself and set out to find Turkey.

I have lingered almost foolishly over this day. But when I recall my childhood, this day always comes back as a type of the very best of it.

I remember I visited Kirsty to ask where Turkey was. She welcomed me as usual, for she was always loving and kind to us. And although I did not visit her so often now, she knew it was because I was more with my father, and had lessons to learn in which she could not assist me. Since I had nothing else to talk about, I told her of Eppie, and how different she had looked when she came out of the house. Kirsty compressed her lips, nodded her head, looked serious, and made me no reply.

Thinking this was strange, I decided to tell Turkey, which otherwise I might not have done. I did not pursue the matter with Kirsty, for I knew her well enough to know that her manner meant that she would say nothing further about it. Having learned where he was, I set out to find him—close by the scene of our adventure with Wandering Willie. I soon came in sight of the cattle feeding, but did not see Turkey.

When I came near the mound, I caught a glimpse of the head of old Mrs. Gregson's cow quietly feeding off the top of the wall from the other side, like an outcast Gentile, while my father's cows, like the favored and greedy Jews, were busy in the short clover inside. Somehow Grannie's cow managed to live in spite of it, and I daresay gave as good milk, though not perhaps quite so much of it, as ill-tempered Hawkie. Mrs. Gregson's granddaughter, however, who did not eat grass, was inside the wall seated on a stone which Turkey had no doubt dragged there for her. Elsie was as usual busy with her knitting. And now I caught sight of Turkey, running from a neighboring cottage with a spade over his shoulder. Elsie had been watching the cows for him.

"What's the matter, Turkey?" I cried, running to meet him.

"Such a wild bees' nest!" answered Turkey. "I'm so glad you've come. I was just thinking whether I should run and fetch you. Elsie and I have been watching them going in and out for the last half hour. Such a lot of bees! There's sure to be a huge store of honey there!"

"But it's too soon to take it," I said. "There'll be a great deal more in a few weeks."

"You're quite right," answered Turkey. "But the nest is by the roadside, and somebody else might find it. And Elsie has never tasted honey all her life, and here she is ready to eat some. And if we take the honey now, the bees will have plenty of time to gather enough for the winter before the flowers are gone. But if we leave it too long they will starve."

I was satisfied with his reasoning.

"But you must keep a sharp lookout for me, Ranald," he said, "for they'll be mad enough. You must keep them off with your cap."

He took off his own cap and gave it to Elsie.

"Here, Elsie, you must look out too," he said, "and keep the bees away. I can tell you a sting is no joke. I've had three myself."

"But what are *you* to do, Turkey?" asked Elsie with an anxious face.

"Oh, Ranald will keep them off me and himself too. I won't pay any attention to them. I must dig away and get at the honey."

With all things thus arranged, Turkey manfully approached the dyke, as they call any kind of wall fence there. In the midst of the grass and moss was one little hole which the bees were going and coming through busily. Turkey put his finger in and felt in what direction the hole went. He judged the position of the hoard of sweet gold, and then struck his shovel with a firm foot into the dyke.

What bees were inside came rushing out in fear and rage, and I had quite enough to do to keep them off our bare heads with my cap. Those who were returning to the hive joined in the defense. But I did my best, and with tolerable success. Elsie stood a little farther back and remained comparatively still, and was thus less the object of their resentment.

In a few moments Turkey had reached the store. Then he began to dig about it carefully to keep from spoiling the honey. First he took out a quantity of cells with nothing in them but the grub-like cradles of the young bees. He threw them away, and went on digging as coolly as if he had been gardening. He left all the defense to me, and I had enough of it and certainly thought mine the harder work of the two!

But now Turkey stooped to the nest, cleared away the earth about it with his hands, and with much care drew out a great piece of honeycomb. Its surface was even and yellow, showing that the cells were full to the brim of the rich store. I can see Turkey in my mind's eye right now, weighing it in his hand, and turning it over to pick away some bits of earth stuck to it before he presented it to Elsie. She sat on her stone like a patient contented queen, waiting for what her subjects would bring her.

"Oh, Turkey! what a piece!" she said as she took it, and opened her pretty mouth and white teeth to have a bite of the treasure.

"Now, Ranald," said Turkey, "we must finish the job before we have any ourselves."

He went on carefully removing the honey, and piling it on the bank. There was not a great deal, because it was so early in the year, and there was not another chunk to equal that he had given Elsie. But when he had got it all out, he said:

"They'll soon find another nest. I don't thing it's any use leaving this open for them. It spoils the dyke too."

As he spoke he began to fill up the hole and beat down the hard earth. Last of all he put in the sod he had first dug away, with the grass and flowers still growing on it. This done, he proceeded to divide what remained of the honey.

"There's a piece for Allister and Davie," he said, "and here's a piece for you, and this for me, and Elsie can take the rest home for herself and Jamie."

Elsie protested at having more, but we both insisted. Turkey got some nice clover and laid the bits of honeycomb in it.

Then we sat and ate our shares, away from the bees, and chatted away for a long time. Turkey and I got up every now and then to look after the cattle, and sometimes Elsie also had to follow her cow when it began looking too longingly on some neighboring field.

But there was plenty of time between watching the cows, and Elsie sang us two or three songs, and Turkey told us one or two stories out of history books he had been reading, and I pulled out my story of the Robins and read to them. And so the hot sun went down in the glowing west, and threw longer and longer shadows eastward. A great shapeless blot of darkness, with legs to it, accompanied every cow and calf and bullock wherever it went. There was a new shadow crop in the grass, and a huge patch with long tree shapes at the end of it stretched away from the foot of the hillock. The weathercock on the top of the church was glistening such a bright gold that it was a wonder it could keep from breaking out into a crow that would rouse all the cocks of the neighborhood, even though they were beginning to get sleepy and thinking of going to roost.

It was time for the cattle, Elsie's cow included, to go home. But just as we rose to break up the assembly, we saw a little girl come flying across the field, as if winged with news. As she came nearer we recognized her. She lived near Mrs. Gregson's cottage, and was one of the little troop whom I had seen pass the manse on their way to gather bilberries.

"Elsie! Elsie!" she cried. "John Adam has taken Jamie. Jamie fell, and John got him."

Elsie looked frightened, but Turkey laughed.

"Never mind, Elsie. John is better than he looks. He won't do him the least harm. He must mind his business, you know."

The Ba' Hill was covered with a young grove of firs, which had trouble growing in that region. It was among their small trunks that the coveted bilberries grew, along with cranberries and crowberries and dwarf junipers. The children of the village were thus attracted to the place, but were no doubt sometimes not too careful over the young trees and sometimes did them damage. Hence, the keeper, John Adam, whose business it was to look after the trees, found it his duty to wage war on the annual hordes of these invaders. And in their eyes Adam was a terrible man.

He was very long and lean, with a flat Roman nose and a rather ill-tempered mouth, while his face was dead white and pitted from smallpox. He always wore a striped nightcap of black and red. The youngsters pretended to determine what kind of a mood he was in by the direction its tassel hung. To them the tassel was a warning, a terror, and a hope.

He could not run very fast, fortunately, for the lean legs were subject to rheumatism, and could take only long but not rapid strides. And if the children had a decent head start, and did not accidentally choose in their terror an impassable direction, they were pretty sure to always get away from him.

Jamie Duff, the most harmless and innocent of creatures who would not have harmed a young fir for anything, did on this occasion take a wrong direction, caught his foot in a hole, fell into a bush, and, nearly paralyzed with terror, was seized by the long fingers of John Adam. He was ignominiously lifted by a portion of his garments. Too frightened to scream or make any resistance, he was borne off as a warning to the rest of the fate which awaited them.

But the character of Adam was not by any means so frightful in Turkey's eyes. He soon succeeded in composing Elsie. He assured her that as soon as he had put up the cattle, he would walk over to Adam's house and try to get Jamie off. Elsie then set off home with her cow, sad but hopeful. She walked away in the light of the red sunset, with her head bent half in trouble, half in attention to her knitting, following her solemn cow, which seemed to take twice as long to get over the ground because she had two pairs of legs instead of one to shuffle across it, dragging her long iron chain with the short stake at the end after her with a gentle clatter over the hard dry road.

I went with Turkey and helped him to fasten up and bed the

cows, went with him and shared his hasty supper of potatoes and oatcake and milk, and then set out refreshed and not in the least afraid in his company, to seek the house of the strange ogre, John Adam.

Chapter Twenty-four

THE UNPLEASANT KEEPER

He had a small farm of his own at the foot of the hill that he was in charge of. It was a poor little place, with a very low thatched cottage. His sister lived there too and kept house for him.

When we approached it, there was no one to be seen. We advanced to the door. I peeped in at the little window as we passed. To my astonishment, I saw Jamie Duff, as I thought, looking quite happy and in the act of lifting a spoon to his mouth.

A moment later, however, I concluded that I must have been mistaken. For when Turkey lifted the latch and we walked in, there were the awful John and his tall sister seated at the table, while poor Jamie was in a corner, with no bowl in his hand and a face that looked dismal and dreary enough. I fancied I caught a glimpse of Turkey laughing in his sleeve, and felt mildly angry with him— for Elsie's sake, I must admit, more than for Jamie's.

"Come in," said Adam, rising. But then seeing who it was, he seated himself again, adding, "Oh, it's you, Turkey!"—Everybody called him Turkey. "Come in and take a spoon."

"No, thank you," said Turkey. "I have had supper. I have only come to ask about that young rascal there."

"Ah, you see him! There he is!" said Adam, looking toward me with an awful expression in his dead brown eyes. "Starving. No home and no supper for him! He'll have to sleep in the hayloft with the rats and mice, and a stray cat or two."

Jamie put his cuffs, the handkerchiefs of the poor, to his eyes. His fate was full of horrors. But again I saw Turkey laughing in his sleeve.

"His sister is very worried about him, Mr. Adam," he said. "Couldn't you let him off this once?"

"On no account. I am entrusted to care for this land, and I must do my duty. The duke has put me in charge of the forest. I have got to look after it."

I could not help thinking what a poor thing it was for a forest. All I knew of forests was from storybooks, and they were full of huge and grand trees. Adam went on.

"And if wicked boys will break down the trees—"

"I only pulled the bilberries," interrupted Jamie, in a whine that went off in a howl.

"James Duff!" said Adam, with awful authority, "I saw you myself tumble over a young larch tree not two feet high."

"The worse for me," sobbed Jamie. "And that was not until you were chasing me."

"Tut! tut! Mr. Adam, the larch tree wasn't a baby," said Turkey. "Let Jamie go. He couldn't help it."

"It was a baby, and it is a baby," said Adam, with a solitary twinkle in the determined dead brown of his eyes. "And I'll have no begging for my good graces here. Transgressors must be prosecuted. And prosecuted he shall be. He shall not get out of this before school time tomorrow morning. He shall be late, too, and I hope the master will whip him well. We must make some examples, you see, Turkey. It's no use you're saying anything. I don't say Jamie's a worse boy than the rest, but he's just as bad; otherwise, how did he come to be here, tumbling over my babies? Answer me that, Master Bannerman?"

He turned and fixed his eyes upon me. I could not meet the awful gaze. My eyes sank before his.

"Example, Master Bannerman, is everything," he went on. "If you do to my trees as this young man has done, I'll serve you the same as I serve him—and that's no sweet service, I'll warrant."

As the keeper ended his little speech, he brought down his fist on the table with such a bang that poor Jamie almost fell off the stool he was sitting on in the corner.

"But let him off just this once," pleaded Turkey, "and I'll personally guarantee that he'll never do it again."

"Oh, as to him, I'm not worried about him," returned the keeper. "But will you be guarantee for the fifty boys that will only make fun of me if I don't make an example of him? I'm in luck to have caught him. No, no, Turkey, it won't do, my man. I'm sorry for his father and his mother, and his sister Elsie, for they're all very good people. But I must make an example of him."

At mention of his family, Jamie burst into another suppressed howl.

"Well, you won't be too hard on him anyhow, will you now?" said Turkey.

"I won't pull his skin over his ears, if that's what you mean," said Adam. "But that's all the promise you'll get out of me."

The tall thin grim sister had sat all the time as if she had no right to be aware of anything that was going on. But her nose, which was more hooked than her brother's, and larger, looked as if in the absence of eyes and ears it was taking notice of everything, and would inform the rest of the senses afterward.

I had a suspicion that the keeper's ferocity was pretended for the occasion, and that he was not such an ogre as I had considered him. Still, the prospect of little Jamie spending the night alone in the loft among the cats and rats was sufficiently dreadful when I thought of my own midnight waking in the barn. There seemed to be no help, however, especially when Turkey rose to say good night.

I felt disconsolate and was not well pleased with how coolly Turkey seemed to be taking the affair. I thought he had not done his best to get Jamie released.

"Poor Elsie!" I said when we got to the road, "she'll be miserable about Jamie."

"Oh no," returned Turkey. "I'll go straight over and tell her. No harm will come to Jamie. John Adam's bark is a good deal worse than his bite. Only I should like to take him home if I could."

It was now twilight, and we walked back to the manse through the glimmering dusk. Turkey left me at the gate and strode on toward the village. As he went, I revolved a new scheme which had arisen in my brain, and for the first time a sense of rivalry with Turkey awoke in my heart.

He did everything for Elsie Duff, and I did nothing. He had robbed the bees' nest for her that very day, and all I had done was partaken in the spoil. Indeed, he had been stung in her service. For though I had done my best, he had received what threatened to be a bad sting on the back of his neck. Now he was going to comfort her about her brother whom he had failed to rescue.

But what if I could succeed where he had failed, and carry the poor boy home in triumph!

As we left the keeper's farm, Turkey had pointed out to me, across the yard, where a small rick or two were standing, the building where Jamie would have to sleep. The loft stood over the cart shed, and was approached by a ladder. Except for the reported rats, to sleep in such a place would be no hardship in weather like this, especially for one who had been brought up as Jamie had.

But I knew that he was a very timid boy, and that I myself would have lain in horror all the night. Therefore, I had been all the way home turning over in my mind what I might be able to do to release him. But whatever I did must be unaided, for I could not count upon Turkey. Nor indeed was it in my heart to share with him the honor of the enterprise that opened before me.

CHAPTER
TWENTY-FIVE
——

A KNIGHT TAKES
TO HIS STEED

I must mention here that my father never objected now to my riding his little mare Missy. Indeed, I had great liberty with regard to her, and took her out for a trot and a gallop as often as I pleased.

Sometimes when there was a press of work she would have to pull a cart or drag a harrow, for she was so handy they could do anything with her. But this did not happen often, and she knew little of actual hard work. My father was very fond of her, and used to tell wonderful stories of her judgment and skill. I believe he was never quite without a hope that somehow or other he should find her again in the next world.

In any event I am certain that it was hard for him to believe that so much wise affection should have been created to be again uncreated. I cannot say that I ever heard him actually say anything of the sort. But where else should I have come by such a firm conviction, dating from a period further back than my memory can reach, that whatever might become of the other horses, Missy was sure to go to heaven?

I had a kind of notion that, being the bearer of my father on all his missions of doctrine and mercy and pastoral care, she belonged to the clergy, and thus shared in their privileges. She must, therefore, I concluded, have a chance of eternity ahead of other animals of her kind. Now that I am grown I am wiser, and extend this hope in my heart to the rest of the horses. For I cannot believe that the God who does nothing in vain ever creates in order to destroy.

I hastened through my lessons for the next day, although my mind was far too full of the adventure before me to concentrate. As soon as prayers and supper were over, about ten o'clock, I crept out of the house and away to the stable.

It was a lovely night. A kind of gray peace filled earth and air and sky. It was not dark, although rather cloudy—only a dim dusk, like a vapor of darkness, floated around everything. I was fond of being out at night, but I had never before ever thought of going so far alone. But with Missy under me I would not feel alone, for she and I were on the best of terms.

I soon managed to open the door of the stable, for I knew where the key lay. It was very dark, but I felt my way through, talking all the time so that the horses wouldn't be startled if I bumped into one of them unexpectedly, for the stable was narrow, and they sometimes lay a good bit out of their stalls. I was careful to speak in a low tone, however, so that the man who slept with only a wooden partition between himself and the stable might not hear.

I soon had the bridle on Missy, but I did not want to waste time in putting on the saddle. I led her out, got on her back with the help of a stone at the stable door, and rode away. She had scarcely been out all day and was rather in the mood for a ride. Andrew's voice, whom the noise of her feet had aroused, came after me, calling to know who it was. I called out in reply and identified myself, for I feared he might rouse the whole place if he thought I was a thief. He went back to his sleep composed, if not contented. In any event, it would have been of no use to follow me.

I had not gone far before the extreme stillness of the night began to sink into my soul and make me quiet. Everything seemed thinking about me, but nothing would tell me what it thought. But since I did not feel I was doing wrong, I was only awed, not frightened by the stillness.

I made Missy slacken her speed, and rode on more gently, in

better harmony with the night. Not a sound broke the silence except the rough cry of the land rail from the fields and the clatter of Missy's feet. I did not like the noise she made, and got upon the grass, for here there was no fence. But the moment she felt the soft grass, off she went at a sudden gallop. Her head was out before I had the least warning of her intention. She tore away over the field in quite another direction from that in which I had been taking her, and the gallop quickened until she was going at her utmost speed.

The rapid flight combined with the darkness—for it seemed like total darkness now—I confess made me frightened. I pulled hard at the reins, but without avail. In a minute or two I had lost my bearings altogether, and could not tell where I was in the field, which was a pretty large one. But soon finding that we were galloping down a hill so steep that I had trouble keeping my seat, I began, not at all to my comfort, to realize in what direction the mare was carrying me.

We were approaching the place where we had sat that same afternoon, close by the mound with the trees on it, the scene of my adventure with Wandering Willie and of the fancied murder. I had scarcely thought of either until the shadows had begun to fall. And now in the night when everything was a shadow, both reflections made it horrible.

Besides, what if Missy should get in the bog! But she knew better than that, wild as her mood was. She avoided it and galloped past, but bore me to a far more frightful goal. Then suddenly she dropped into a canter, and then a moment later stood stock-still.

We were in front of a cottage half in ruins, occupied by an old woman whom I dimly recollected. I had gone to see her once with my father—a good many years ago, as it appeared to me then. Old Betty was still alive, however very old, and bedridden. I remembered that from the top of her wooden bed hung a rope for her to pull herself up by when she wanted to turn over, for she was very rheumatic. And for some reason or other this rope had filled me with horror.

But there was more of the same sort. The cottage had once served as a blacksmith's shop, and the bellows had been left in its place. Now there is nothing particularly frightful about a pair of bellows, however large it may be. And yet the recollection of that huge structure of wood and leather, with the great iron nose projecting from the contracting cheeks of it, at the head of the old woman's bed, so capable yet so useless, did return upon me with terror in the dusk of that lonely night. It was mingled with a vague suspicion that the old woman was a bit of a witch, and a very doubtful memory that she had been seen on one occasion by some night traveler when a frightful storm was raging, blowing away at that very bellows as hard as her skinny arms and lean body could work it, so that there was almost as great a storm of wind in her little room as there was outside of it.

If there was any truth in the story, it is easily explained by the fact that the poor old woman had been a little out of her mind for many years—and no wonder, for she was nearly a hundred, they said. Neither is it any wonder that when Missy stopped almost suddenly, with her forefeet and her neck stretched forward, and her nose pointed straight for the door of the cottage at a few yards' distance, that I should have felt very strange indeed. Whether my hair stood on end or not I do not know, but I certainly did feel my skin creep all over me.

An ancient elder tree grew at one end of the cottage, and I heard the lonely sigh of a little breeze through its branches. The next instant a frightful sound from within the cottage broke the night air into what seemed a universal shriek.

Missy gave a plunge, turned round on her hind legs, and tore from the place. I very nearly lost my seat, but terror made me cling all the harder to my companion as she flew home.

It hardly took her a minute to reach the stable door. There she had to stop, for I had shut it myself. It was humiliating to find myself there instead of under John Adam's hayloft, the rescuer of Jamie Duff. But I did not think of that for a while.

Shaken with terror, and afraid to dismount, I called out to Andrew as well as my fear would permit. But I could hardly manage my voice, and I could do little more than howl with it.

In a few minutes—a time that seemed to me of awful duration, for who could tell what might be following me up from the hollow?—Andrew appeared half dressed, and not in the best of tempers. It was an odd thing, he remarked, to go out riding when honest people were in their beds. Hearing his voice, and made more communicative by the trial I had gone through, I told him the whole story, what I had intended to do, and how I had been frustrated.

He listened, scratched his head, and said someone ought to see if anything was the matter with the old woman. Then he turned in to put on the rest of his clothes.

"You had better go home to bed, Ranald," he said.

"Won't you be frightened, Andrew?" I asked.

"Frightened? What should I be frightened at? It's all a waste to be frightened before you know whether the thing is worth it."

My courage had been quickly coming back to me in the warm presence of another human being. I was still seated on Missy. To go home having done nothing for Jamie, and therefore for Elsie, after all my grand ideas of rescue, was too mortifying! And yet suppose the something which gave the fearful cry in the cottage should be out roaming the fields and looking for me!

I had courage enough, however, to remain where I was till Andrew came out again, and as I sat on the mare's back, my courage gradually continued to rise. Nothing increases terror so much as running away.

"What do you think it could be, Andrew?" I asked him when he reappeared.

"How should I tell?" returned Andrew. "The old woman has a very queer cock, I know, that always roosts on the top of her bed and crows like no rooster I ever heard crow. Or it might be Wandering Willie—he goes to see her sometimes, and the demented creature might strike up his pipes at any unearthly hour."

I was not satisfied with either suggestion. But the sound I had heard had already grown so indistinct in my memory that for anything I could tell, it might have been either. The terror which it woke in my mind had made me unable to make any observations or set down any facts regarding it. I could only remember that I had heard a frightful noise. But as to what it was like, I could not say a thing.

I begged Andrew to put the saddle on for me, as I would then have more command of Missy. He went and got it. He did not seem to be at all overanxious about old Betty. In the meantime I buckled on an old rusty spur that lay in the stable window, the leathers of it crumbling off in flakes.

Thus armed, and mounted with my feet in the stirrups, and therefore with a good pull on Missy's mouth, I found my courage once more equal to the task before me. Andrew and I parted at right angles. He went across the field to old Betty's cottage, and I once more took to the road in the direction of John Adam's farm.

—

ATTEMPTED RESCUE

It must now have been about eleven o'clock.

The clouds had cleared off and the night had changed from brown and gray to blue sparkling with gold. I could see much better and fancied I could hear better too. But neither advantage did much for me.

I had not ridden far from the stable before I again found myself very much alone and unprotected, with only the wide, silent fields about me, and the wider and more silent sky over my head.

The fear began to return. I imagined something strange creeping along every ditch—something shapeless, but with a terrible cry in it. Next, I thought I saw a scarcely visible form—now like a creature on all fours, now like a man, far off, but coming rapidly toward me across the nearest field. It always vanished, however, before it came close.

The worst of it was that the faster I rode, the more frightened I became. For my speed seemed to draw the terrors all the faster after me. Once I discovered this I changed my plan. When I felt more frightened, I drew rein and went slower. This was to throw a sort of defiance to the fear, and certainly as often as I did so it lessened. Fear is a worse thing than danger.

I had to pass very near the pool to which Turkey and I had gone the night of our adventure with Bogbonny's bull. That story was now far off in the past, but I did not relish the full shine of the water in the hollow in any case. In fact, I owed the greater part of the courage I possessed—and it was little enough for my needs—to Missy. I would not have dared gone on such a midnight journey on my own two legs. It was not that I could so easily run away with four instead, but that somehow I was lifted above the ordinary level of fear by being upon her back. I think many men draw their courage out of their horses.

At length I came in sight of the keeper's farm. And just at that moment the moon peeped out from behind a hill, throwing as long shadows as the setting sun, but in the other direction. The shadows were very different too. Somehow they were more like the light that made them than the sun shadows are to the sunlight. Both the light and the shadows of the moon were strange and fearful to me. The sunlight and its shadows are all so strong and so real and so friendly, you seem to know all about them; and they belong to your house, and they sweep all fear and dismay out of honest people's hearts. But with the moon and its shadows it is very different indeed.

The fact is, the moon is trying to do what she cannot do. She is trying to dispel a great sun shadow—for the night is just the gathering into one mass of all the shadows of the sun. The moon is not strong enough for this, for her light is not her own. It is secondhand light from the sun himself, and her shadows are therefore also secondhand shadows, pieces cut out of the great sun shadow, and colored a little with the moon's yellowness.

If I were writing for grown people I should tell them that those who understand things because they think about them, and ask God to teach them, walk in the sunlight. And others, who take things because other people tell them so, are always walking in the strange moonlight, and are subject to no end of stumbles and terrors, for they hardly know light from darkness.

Well, at first the moon frightened me a little—she looked so knowing and yet all she said round about me was so strange. But I rode quietly up to the back of the yard where the ricks stood, got off Missy and fastened the bridle to the gate, and walked across to the cart shed, where the moon was shining upon the ladder leading up to the loft.

I climbed the ladder, and after several failures succeeded in finding how the door was fastened. When I opened it, the moonlight got in before me. It poured in all at once upon a heap of straw in the farthest corner, where Jamie was lying asleep with a rug over him.

I crossed the floor, knelt down by him, and tried to wake him. This was not so easy. He was far too sound asleep to be troubled by the rats, for sleep is an armor—yes, a castle—against many enemies. I got hold of one of his hands, and in lifting it to pull him up found a cord tied to his wrist.

I was indignant: they had tied him up like a thief! I gave the cord a great tug of anger, pulled out my knife, and cut it. Then I hauled Jamie up, and got him half awake at last. He started with fright first, and then began to cry. As soon as he was awake enough to know me, he stopped crying but not staring. His eyes seemed to have nothing more than moonlight in them.

"Come along, Jamie," I said. "I've come to take you home."

"I don't want to go home," said Jamie. "I want to go to sleep again."

"That's very ungrateful of you, Jamie," I said, full of my own importance, "when I've come so far in the middle of the night to set you free."

"I'm free enough," said Jamie. "I had a much better supper than I should have had at home. I don't want to go before the morning."

He began to whimper again.

"Do you call this free?" I said, holding up his wrist where the end of the cord was hanging.

"Oh," said Jamie, "that's only—"

But before he got further, the moonlight in the loft was darkened. I looked hurriedly toward the door. There stood the strangest figure with the moon behind it. I thought at first it was the Kelpie come after me, for it was a tall woman.

My heart gave a great jump up, but I swallowed it down. I would not disgrace myself in front of Jamie. It was not the Kelpie, however, but the keeper's sister, the great, grim, gaunt woman I had seen at the table at supper. I will not attempt to describe her appearance. It was peculiar enough, for she had just got out of bed and thrown an old shawl about her. She was not pleasant to look at.

I had, in fact, waked her myself. For as Jamie explained to me afterward, the cord that was tied to his wrist, instead of being meant to keep him a prisoner, was a devise of her kindness to keep him from being too frightened. The other end had been tied to her wrist so that if anything happened, he might pull her and then she would come to him.

"What's the matter, Jamie Duff?" she said in a gruff voice.

I stood up as bravely as I could.

"It's only me, Miss Adam," I said.

"And who are you?" she returned.

"Ranald Bannerman," I answered.

"Oh," she said in a puzzled tone. "What are you doing here at this time of the night?"

"I came to take Jamie home, but he won't go."

"You're a silly boy to think my brother John would do him any harm," she returned. "You're comfortable enough, aren't you, Jamie Duff?"

"Yes, thank you, ma'am, quite comfortable," said Jamie, who was now wide awake. "But please, ma'am, Ranald didn't mean any harm."

"He's a housebreaker though," she replied with a grim chuckle, "and he'd better go home again as fast as he can. If John Adam should come out, I don't exactly know what might happen. Or perhaps he'd like to stay and keep you company."

"No, thank you, Miss Adam," I said. "I will go home."

"Come along, then, and let me shut the door after you."

Somewhat irritated with Jamie Duff's indifference to my well-meaning attempt to rescue him, I followed her without even telling him good night.

"Oh, you've got Missy, have you?" she said, spying her where she stood. "Would you like a drink of milk or a piece of oatcake before you go?"

"No, thank you," I said. "I shall be glad to go to bed."

"I should think so," she answered. "Jamie is quite comfortable, I assure you, and I'll be sure he's in time for school in the morning. There's no harm in him, poor thing!"

She undid the bridle for me, helped me to mount in the kindest way, said good night, and stood looking after me till I was some distance off. I went home at a good gallop, took off the saddle and bridle and laid them in a cart in the shed, turned Missy loose into the stable, shut the door, and ran across the field to the manse, wanting nothing but my bed.

When I came near the house from the back, I saw a figure entering the gate from the front. It was in the full light of the moon, which was now up a good way. Before it had reached the door I had got behind the next corner, and peeping round saw that my first impression was correct. It was the Kelpie.

She entered, and closed the door behind her very softly. Afraid of being locked out, a danger which had scarcely occurred to me before, I hastened after her. But finding the door already locked, I called through the keyhole. She gave a cry of alarm, but after a moment opened the door, looking pale and frightened.

"What are you doing out-of-doors at this time of night?" she asked, but without quite her usual arrogance. Although she tried to put it on, her voice trembled too much for it.

I turned the question back on her. "What were you doing out yourself?" I said.

"Looking after you, of course."

"That's why you locked the door, I suppose—to keep me out."

She had no answer ready, but looked as if she would have hit me. "I shall let your father know of your goings-on," she said, recovering herself a little.

"You need not trouble. I shall tell him at breakfast in the morning. You had better tell him too."

I said this, not that I did not believe she had been out to look for me, but because I thought she had locked the door to annoy me. So I took my revenge in being rude. Doors were seldom locked during the summer nights in that part of the country. She made me no reply, but turned and left me, not even shutting the door.

I closed it, and went to bed weary enough.

CHAPTER
TWENTY-SEVEN

—

TURKEY'S PLOT

The next day at breakfast I told my father all the previous day's adventures. Never since he had so kindly rescued me from the misery of wickedness had I kept a single thing from him. He gave us every freedom, yet expected us to speak openly and frankly about our doings. To have been unwilling to let him know something would have revealed that it was already a thing we disapproved of ourselves. And nothing of the kind had yet occurred with me since the Peter Mason affair.

Hence it came that as I grew older I seemed to come nearer my father. He was to us like a wiser and more beautiful self over us—a more enlightened conscience, always lifting us up toward its own higher self.

This was Sunday. My father was not so strict in his ideas concerning the day as most of his parishioners. So long as we were sedate and orderly, and did not laugh nor talk *too* loud, he seldom interfered with our behavior or tried to change the direction of our conversation.

He did not, like some people, require or expect us to care about religious things as much as he did. We could not yet know as he did what they really were. But he was a little more strict, I think, about bringing the standard of right to bear upon things on Sunday than on other days. I believe he thought that to order our ways was our best preparation for receiving higher instruction afterward. For one thing, we should then, upon failure, feel the burden of it the more, and be the more ready to repent and seek the forgiveness of God, and that best help of his which at length makes a man good within himself.

He listened attentively to my story, seemed puzzled at the cry I had heard from the cottage, said nothing could have gone very wrong, or we should have heard of it, especially as Andrew had gone to investigate, and then laughed over the appearance of Miss Adam and my failure in rescuing Jamie Duff.

He said, however, that I had no right to interfere with constituted authority—that Adam was put there to protect the trees, and even if he had got hold of a harmless person, Jamie was certainly trespassing, and I ought to have been satisfied with Turkey's way of looking after the matter.

I saw that my father was right. And a little further thought convinced me that the deepest root in my conduct was my desire to show off to Jamie Duff's sister. I suspect that almost all silly actions have their root in selfishness, whether it take the form of vanity, conceit, greed, or ambition.

While I was telling my tale, Mrs. Mitchell kept coming into the room oftener, and lingering longer, than usual. I did not think of this till afterward. I said nothing about her, for I saw no reason to. But I do not doubt she was afraid I would and wanted to be close at hand to defend herself. She was a little more friendly to me in church that day. She always sat beside little Davie.

When we came out, I saw Andrew and hurried after him to hear how he had spent the night before. He told me he had found all perfectly quiet at the cottage, except the old woman's cough, which was troublesome, and gave proof that she was alive, and probably as well as usual. He suggested the noise was all in my imagination at which I was duly indignant, and asked him if it was also Missy's fancy that made her go off like a mad creature. He then returned to his former idea of a rooster, and since this did not insult my dignity, I let it pass. I leaned myself, however, to the notion of Wandering Willie's pipes.

On the following Wednesday we had a half holiday, and before

dinner I went to find Turkey at the farm. He met me in the yard and took me into the barn.

"I want to talk to you, Ranald," he said.

I remember so well how the barn looked that day. The upper half of one of the doors had a hole in it, and a long pencil of sunlight streamed in, falling like a pool of glory upon a heap of yellow straw. So golden grew the straw beneath it that the spot looked as if it were the source of the shine, and sent the slanting ray up and out of the hole in the door. We sat down beside it. I wondered why

Turkey looked so serious and important, for it was unlike him.

"Ranald," said Turkey, "I can't bear that the master should have bad people about him."

"What do you mean?" I asked.

"I mean the Kelpie."

"She's a nasty thing, I know," I answered. "But my father considers her a faithful servant."

"That's just it. She is not faithful. I've suspected her for a long time. She's so rough and ill-tempered that she looks honest. But I shall be able to show her up yet. You wouldn't call it honest to cheat the poor, would you?"

"I should think not. But what do you mean?"

"There must have been something to put old Eppie in such an ill temper on Saturday, don't you think?"

"I suppose she had a sting from the Kelpie's tongue."

"No, Ranald, that's not it. I had heard whispers going about. And last Saturday, after we came home from John Adam's, and after I had told Elsie about Jamie, I ran up the street to old Eppie. You would have got nothing out of her, for she wouldn't have wanted to tell you. But she told me all about it."

"What a creature you are, Turkey! Everybody tells you everything."

"I don't think I am such a gossip as that, Ranald. But when you have a chance, you ought to set right whatever you can. Right is the most important thing, Ranald."

"But aren't you afraid they'll call you a meddler, Turkey? Not that *I* think so, for I'm sure if you do anything against anybody, it would be *for* some other body."

"That would be no justification if I wasn't in the right," said Turkey. "But I'm willing to bear any blame that comes of it. And I wouldn't meddle for anybody who could take care of himself. But neither old Eppie nor your father can do that. The one's too poor, the other's too good."

"I *was* wondering what you meant by saying my father couldn't take care of himself."

"He's too good, Ranald. He believes in everybody. *I* wouldn't have kept that Kelpie in *my* house half the time he has."

"Did you ever say anything to Kirsty about her?"

"I did once. But she told me to mind my own business. Kirsty snubs me because I laugh at her stories. But Kirsty is as good as gold, and I wouldn't mind if she boxed my ears—as indeed she's done many a time."

"But what's the Kelpie been doing to old Eppie?"

"First of all, Eppie has been playing her a trick."

"Then she mustn't complain."

"Eppie's was a lawful trick, though. The old women have been laying their old heads together."

"I don't understand you a bit."

"Then I'll begin at the beginning. There has been for some time a growing conviction among the poor folk that the Kelpie never gives them an honest handful of meal when they go their rounds. But this was very hard to prove, and although they all suspected it, few of them were absolutely certain about it. So they resolved that some of them should go with empty bags. Every one of those found a full handful at the bottom. Still they were not satisfied. They said she was the one to take care what she was about. So old Eppie decided to go with something at the bottom of her bag to look like a good quantity of meal already gathered. The moment the door was closed behind her—that was last Saturday—she peeped into the bag. Not one grain of meal was to be discovered. That was why she passed you muttering to herself and looking so angry. Now it will never do that the manse, of all places, where the minister himself lives, should be the one where the poor people are cheated of their rightful supply of meal. But we must have yet better proof than this before we can say anything."

"What do you mean to do, Turkey?" I asked. "Why do you suppose she does it? It can't be for the sake of saving my father's meal. He has plenty to spare."

"No, she must do something with it, and, I suppose convinces herself that she is not stealing—only saving it from the poor, and so making a right to it for herself. I can't help thinking that her being out that same night had something to do with it. Did you ever know her to go see old Betty?"

"No. She doesn't like her. I know that."

"I'm not so sure. She pretends perhaps. But we'll have a try. I think I can outwit her. She's fair game, you know."

"How? What will you do? Do tell me, Turkey," I cried eagerly.

"Not today. I will tell you when it is time."

He got up and went about his work.

Chapter Twenty-eight

OLD JOHN JAMIESON

A s I returned to the house, I met my father.

"Well, Ranald, what are you about?" he said, in his usual gentle tone.

"Nothing in particular, Father," I answered.

"Well, I am going to see an old man—John Jamieson—I don't think you know him. He has not been able to come to church for a long time. They tell me he is dying. Would you like to go with me?"

"Yes, Father. But won't you take Missy?"

"Not if you will walk with me. It's only about three miles."

"Very well, Father. I would like to go with you."

On the way my father talked about various things. I remember in particular he talked about the sound and the look of poetry, and how the sound was the most important even though it was often overlooked.

"The eye sees only the sense of a poem," he said; "the ear sees the shape of it. To judge poetry without heeding the sound of it is nearly as bad as to judge a rose by smelling it with your eyes shut. Every poem carries its own tune in its own heart, and to read it aloud is the only way to bring out its tune."

I enjoyed all kinds of poems so much better after that.

"The right way of anything," said my father, "may be called the tune of it. We have to find out the tune of our own lives. Some people don't seem ever to find it out, and so their lives are a broken and uncomfortable thing to them—full of ups and downs and disappointments, and never going as it was meant to go."

"But what is the right tune of a person's life, Father?"

"The will of God, my boy."

"But how is a person to know that, Father?"

"By trying to do what he knows of it already. Everybody has a different kind of tune in his life, and no one can find out another's tune for him, though he *may* help him to find it for himself."

"But aren't we to read the Bible, Father?"

"Yes, if it's in order to obey it. To read the Bible thinking to please God by the mere reading of it is to think like a heathen."

"And aren't we to say our prayers, Father?"

"We are to ask God for what we want. If we don't want something, we are only acting like pagans to speak as if we did, and call it a prayer and think we are pleasing him."

I was silent.

"I fancy the old man we are going to see found out the tune of *his* life long ago," my father resumed.

"Is he a very wise man then?"

"That depends on what you mean by *wise*. I should call him a wise man, for to find out one's tune is the truest wisdom. But he's not a learned or educated man at all. I doubt if he ever read a book but the Bible, except perhaps *Pilgrim's Progress*. I believe he has always been very fond of that one. *You* like it too—don't you, Ranald?"

"I've read it several times, Father. But I was a little tired of it before I got through it last time."

"But you did read it through, did you? The last time, I mean?"

"Oh yes, Father. I never like to leave the loose end of a thing hanging about."

"That's right, my boy, that's right. Well, I think you'd better not open the book again for a long time—say twenty years at least. It's a great deal too good a book to let yourself get tired of. By that time I trust you will be able to understand it much better than you can at present."

I felt a little sorry that I would not be able to look at *Pilgrim's Progress* for twenty years. But I am very glad for his advice now.

"We don't want to spoil good things by letting ourselves get tired of them," my father added. "We should get tired of the sunlight itself, beautiful as it is, if God did not send it away every night. We're not even fit to have the moonlight always. The moon is buried in the darkness every month. And because we can bear nothing for any length of time together, we are sent to sleep every night, so that we may begin fresh in the morning."

"I see, Father," I answered.

We talked on until we came in sight of John Jamieson's cottage.

What a poor little place it was to look at—built of clay, which had hardened in the sun till it was just one solid brick! But it was a better place to live in than it looked, for no wind could come through the walls, although there was plenty of wind about. Three little windows looked eastward to the rising sun, and one to the south. It stood on the side of a heathy hill, which rose up steep behind it, and bending round sheltered it from the north. A low wall of loose stones enclosed a small garden, reclaimed from the hill, where grew some vegetables and cabbages and potatoes, with a flower here and there in between. In summer it was pleasant enough, for the warm sun makes any place pleasant. But in winter it must have been a cold, dreary place indeed. There was no other house within sight of it. A little brook went cantering down the hill close to the end of the cottage, singing merrily.

"It is a long way to the sea, but by its very nature the water will find it at last," said my father, pointing to the stream as we crossed it by the single stone that was its bridge.

He had to bend his head low to enter the cottage. An old woman, the sick man's wife, rose from the side of the chimney to greet us. My father asked how John was.

"Wearing away" was her answer. "But he'll be glad to see you."

We turned in the direction in which her eyes guided us. The first thing I saw was a small withered-looking head, and the next a withered-looking hand, large and bony. The old man lay in a bed closed in with boards, so that very little light fell upon him, but his hair glistened silvery through the gloom. My father drew a chair beside him. John looked up, and seeing who it was, feebly held out his hand. My father took it and stroked it.

"Well, John, my man," he said, "you've had a hard life of it."

"No harder than I could bear," said John.

"It's a grand thing to be able to say that," said my father.

"Oh, for that matter, I would go through it all again if it was *his* will, and willingly. I have no will but his, sir."

"Well, John, I wish we could all say the same. When a man comes to that, the Lord lets him have what he wants. What do you want now, John?"

"To depart and be with the Lord. It wouldn't be true, sir, to say that I wasn't weary. It seems to me, if it's the Lord's will, I've had enough of this life. Even if death be a long sleep, as some people say, till the judgment, I think I would rather sleep, for I'm very weary. Only there's the old woman there! I don't like the thought of leaving her."

"But you can trust God for her too, can't you?"

"It would be a poor thing if I couldn't, sir."

"Were you ever hungry, John—dreadfully hungry, I mean?"

"Never longer than I could bear," he answered. "When you think it's the will of God, hunger doesn't get much hold of you, sir."

"You must excuse me, John, for asking so many questions. You know God better than I do, and I want my young man here to know how strong the will of God makes a man, old or young. He needn't care about anything else, need he?"

"There's nothing else to care about, sir. If only the will of God be done, everything's all right, you know. I do believe, sir, that God cares more for me than my old woman herself does, and she's been as good a wife to me as ever was. Young gentleman, you know that God numbers the very hairs of our heads? There's not many of mine left to number," he added with a faint smile, "but there's plenty of yours. You mind the will of God, and he'll look after you. That's the way he divides the business of life."

I saw now that my father's talk as we came had been to prepare me for what John Jamieson would say. I cannot pretend, however, to have understood the old man at the time, but his words have often come back to me since, and helped me through some pretty severe trials; although, like the old man said, I have never found any of them too hard to bear.

"Have you no children to come and help your wife to take care of you?" my father asked.

"I've had ten, sir, but only three are left alive. There'll be plenty to welcome me home when I go. One of the three's in Canada, and can't come. Another's in Australia, and he can't come. But Maggie's not far off, and she's got leave from her mistress to come for a week—only we don't want her to come till I'm nearer my end. I should like her to see the last of her old father, for I shall be young again by the next time she sees me, please God. He's all in all—isn't he, sir?"

"True, John. If we have God, we have all things, for all things are his and we are his. But we mustn't weary you too much. Thank you very much for your good advice."

"I beg your pardon, sir. I had no intention of speaking like that. I never could give advice in all my life. I always found it was as much as I could do to take the good advice that was given to me. I should like to be prayed for in the church next Sunday, sir, if you please."

"But can't you pray for yourself, John?"

"Yes, sir, but I would like to have some spiritual gift because my friends asked it for me. Let them pray for more faith for me. I want more and more of that. The more you have, the more you want. Don't you, sir? And I might not ask enough for myself, now that I'm so old and so tired. I sleep a great deal, sir."

"Then don't you think God will take care to give you enough, even if you shouldn't ask for enough?" said my father.

"No doubt of that. But you see I am able to think of it now, and so I must put things in a train for the time when I won't be able to think of it."

Something like this was what John said. And although I could not understand it then, my father spoke to me several times about it afterward, and I came to see how the old man wanted to provide against the evil time by starting prayers heavenward beforehand, as it were.

My father prayed by his bedside, pulled a package or two from his pocket for his wife, and then we walked home together in silence. My father was not the man to pile words upon words and so smother the thought that lay in them. He had taken me for the sake of the lesson I might receive, and he left it to strike root in my mind, which he judged more likely if it remained undisturbed.

CHAPTER
TWENTY-NINE
———

TURKEY'S TRICK

When we came to the farm on our way home, we looked in to see Kirsty, but found the key in the door, indicating that she had gone out. As we left the yard, we saw a strange-looking woman, to all appearance a beggar, approaching. She had a bag over her shoulder and walked stooped with her eyes on the ground, not even lifting them to greet us. This sort of behavior rarely showed itself in our parish.

My father took little notice, but I could not help turning back to look after the woman. To my surprise she stood looking after us, but the moment I turned, she turned also and walked on. When I looked again, she had vanished. I thought she must have gone into the farmyard.

Not liking the look of her, and remembering that Kirsty was gone, I asked my father if I had not better see if any of the men were about the stable. He approved and I ran back to the house.

The door was still locked. I called Turkey, and heard him reply from one of the farthest of the cowhouses. I ran to it and told him my story. He asked if my father knew I had come back. I said he did. He threw down his pitchfork and hastened with me. We searched every house and barn and shed about the place, but could find no sign whatever of the woman.

157

"Are you sure it wasn't your imagination, Ranald?" said Turkey.

"Quite sure. Ask my father. She passed as near us as you are to me now."

Turkey hurried away to search the hayloft once more, but without success, and at last I heard my father calling me.

I ran to him and told him there was no woman to be seen.

"That's odd," he said. "She must have passed straight through the yard and got out at the other side before you went in. While you were looking for her, she was no doubt plodding away out of sight. Come along, and let us have our tea."

I could not feel quite satisfied about it, but as there was no other explanation, I persuaded myself that my father was right.

The next Saturday evening I was in the nursery with my brothers. It was growing dusk when I heard a knocking. Mrs. Mitchell did not seem to hear it, so I went and opened the door.

There was the same beggar woman. Rather frightened, I called aloud, and Mrs. Mitchell came. When she saw it was a beggar, she went back and reappeared with a wooden basin filled with meal. She took from it a handful as she came, in what looked like preparation for dropping it in the customary way into the woman's bag. Mrs. Mitchell put her hand through the opening of the bag, then withdrew it a moment later. The woman never spoke, but closed the mouth of her bag and turned away.

Curiosity gave me courage to follow her. She walked with long strides in the direction of the farm. I kept at a little distance behind her. She made for the yard.

As soon as she entered it, I ran as fast as I could, and just caught sight of her back as she went into one of the cowhouses. I darted after her. She turned round upon me—fiercely, I thought. But then imagine my surprise when she held out the open mouth of the bag toward me and said:

"Not one grain, Ranald! Put in your hand and feel."

It was Turkey.

I stared in amazement, unable for a moment to get rid of the ghost of the woman in the reality of Turkey's presence. He burst out laughing at my perplexed stare.

"Why didn't you tell me before, Turkey?" I asked, able at length to join in the laugh.

"Because then you would have had to tell your father, and I did not want him to be troubled about it, at least before we had got things clear. I always *did* wonder how he could keep such a creature about him."

"He doesn't know her as we do, Turkey."

"No, she never gives him the chance. But now, Ranald, couldn't you manage to find out whether she makes any store of the meal she pretends to give away to the poor?"

A thought struck me.

"I heard Davie the other day asking her why she had two meal tubs. Perhaps that has something to do with it."

"You must find out. Don't ask Davie."

For the first time it occurred to me that the Kelpie had upon that night of terror been out on business of her own, and had not been looking for me at all.

"Then she was down at old Betty's cottage," said Turkey when I told him of my suspicion, "and Wandering Willie was there too, and Andrew must have been right about the pipes. Willie hasn't once been to the house since he took Davie. She has no doubt gone to meet him at Betty's. Depend on it, Ranald, he's her brother, or nephew, or something, as I always used to say. I do believe she gives him the meal to take home to her family somewhere. Did you ever hear anything about her friends?"

"I never heard her speak of any."

"Then I don't believe they're respectable. I don't, Ranald. But it will be a great trouble to the minister to have to turn her away. I wonder if we couldn't contrive to make her go of herself. I wish we could scare her out of the country. It's not nice either for a woman like that to have to do with such innocents as Allister and Davie."

"She's very fond of Davie."

"So she is. That's the only good thing I know of her. But hold your tongue, Ranald, till we find out more."

Acting on the hint Davie had given me, I soon discovered the second meal tub. It was small and carefully stowed away. It was now nearly full, and every day I watched in the hope that when she emptied it, I should be able to find out what she did with the meal. But Turkey's suggestion about frightening her away kept working in my brain.

159

CHAPTER

THIRTY

——

My Own Schemes

I began a series of persecutions of the Kelpie on my own. I was doubtful whether Turkey would approve of them, so I did not tell him for some time. But I was ambitious of showing him that I could do something without him. It is probably not necessary to relate the silly tricks I played on her—my father made me sorry enough for them afterward. My only excuse is that I hoped by them to drive the Kelpie away.

There was a closet in the hall. Its floor was directly over the Kelpie's bed, with no ceiling in between. With a gimlet I bored a hole in the floor. Then I passed a bit of string through it. I had already got a bit of black cloth and sewed and stuffed into it something of the shape of a rat. Watching for an opportunity, I tied this to the end of the string by the head, and hid it under her pillow.

When she was going to bed, I went into the closet and laid my mouth to the floor, then began squeaking like a rat and scratching with my nails. Knowing by the exclamations she made that I had attracted her attention, I tugged at the string. This lifted the pillow a little, and of course out came my rat.

I heard her scream and open her door. I pulled the rat tight up to the ceiling. Then the door of the nursery, where we slept only in the winter, opened and shut, and I concluded that she had gone

160

to bed there to avoid the rat. I could hardly sleep for pleasure at my success.

As she waited on us at breakfast the next morning, she told us that she had seen in her bed the biggest rat she ever saw in all her life, and had not had a wink of sleep because of it.

"Well," said my father, "that comes of not liking cats. You should get a pussy to take care of you."

She grumbled something and left.

She changed her room to the nursery. But there it was yet easier to plague her. Having observed in which bed she lay, I passed the string with the rat at the end of it over the middle of a bar that ran across just above her head, then took the string along the top of the other bed, and through a little hole in the door. As soon as I judged her safe in bed, I dropped the rat with a plump.

It must have fallen on or very near her face. I heard her give a loud cry. But before she could reach the door, I had fastened the string to a nail and got out of the way.

It was not so easy in those days to get a light, for the earliest form of match was only just making its appearance in that part of the country, and was very expensive. Therefore, she had to go to the kitchen, where the fire never went out, summer or winter. Afraid that on her return she would search the bed and find my harmless animal suspended by the neck, and then descend upon me with all the wrath from her needless terror, I crept into the room, got down my rat, pulled away the string, and escaped.

The next morning she said nothing about the rat, but went to a neighbor's and brought home a fine cat. I laughed in my sleeve, thinking how little her cat could protect her from my rat.

Once more, however, she changed her quarters and went into a sort of inferior spare room in the upper part of the house. This suited my operations still better, for from my own bed I could now manage to drop and pull up the rat, drawing it away beyond the danger of discovery. The next night she took the cat into the room with her, and for that one night I judged it prudent to leave her alone. But the next, having secured Kirsty's cat, I turned him into the room after she was in bed. The result was a frightful explosion of feline wrath.

I now thought I might boast of my successes to Turkey, but he was not pleased.

"She is sure to find you out, Ranald," he said, "and then whatever else we do will be a failure. Leave her alone till we have her well in our power."

I do not care to linger over this part of my story. I am a little ashamed of it.

We found at length that her private reservoir was quite full of meal. I kept close watch, and finding one night that she was not in the house, I discovered also that the meal tub was now empty. I ran to Turkey, and together we hurried to Betty's cottage.

It was a cloudy night, with glimpses of moonlight. When we reached the place, we heard voices talking, and were satisfied that both the Kelpie and Wandering Willie were there.

"We must wait till she comes out," said Turkey. "We must be able to say we saw her."

There was a great stone standing out of the ground not far from the door, just opposite the elder tree, and the path lay between them.

"You get behind that tree—no, you are the smaller—you get behind that stone and I'll get behind the tree," said Turkey. "When the Kelpie comes out, you make a noise like a beast, and rush at her on all fours."

"I'm good at a pig," I said. "Will a pig do?"

"Yes, well enough."

"But what if she knows me, and catches me, Turkey?"

"She will jump away from you to my side. I shall rush out like a mad dog, and then she'll run for it."

We waited a long time—a very long time, it seemed to me. It was good it was summer. We talked a little across the path, and that helped to pass the weary time, but at last I said in a whisper:

"Let's go home, Turkey, and lock the doors and just keep her out."

"You go home then, Ranald, and I'll wait. I don't mind if it be till tomorrow morning. It's not enough to be sure ourselves, we must be able to make other people sure."

"I'll wait as long as you do, Turkey. Only I'm very sleepy, and she might come out when I'm asleep."

"I shall keep you awake!" replied Turkey, and we settled down again for a while.

At long last the latch of the door was lifted. I was just falling asleep, but the sound brought me wide awake at once. I peeped from behind my shelter. It was the Kelpie, with an empty bag—a pillowcase, I believe, in her hand. Behind her came Wandering Willie, but did not follow her from the door. The moment was favorable, for the moon was under a thick cloud.

Just as she reached the stone, I rushed out on hands and knees, grunting and squeaking like a very wild pig indeed. As Turkey had foretold, she darted aside, and I retreated behind my stone. The same instant Turkey rushed at her with such a canine fury that the imitation startled even me, who had expected it. You would have thought the animal was ready to tear a whole army to pieces with such a complication of fierce growls and barks and squeals that he darted on the unfortunate culprit.

She took to her heels at once, not daring to make for the cottage, because the enemy was behind her. But I had hardly got behind the stone again, repressing my laughter with all my might, when I was seized from behind by Wandering Willie, who had no fear either of pig or dog. He began beating me.

"Turkey! Turkey!" I cried.

The cry stopped his barking pursuit of the Kelpie. He jumped to his feet and rushed to my aid. But when he saw the state of affairs, he turned at once for the cottage.

"Now for a kick at the bagpipes!" he cried.

Wandering Willie was not too much a fool to remember and understand. He left me instantly and made for the cottage. Turkey drew back and let him enter, then closed the door and held it.

"Get away, Ranald. I can run faster than Willie. You'll be out of sight in a few yards."

But instead of coming after us, Wandering Willie began playing a most triumphant tune on his darling bagpipes. How the poor old woman enjoyed it, I do not know. Perhaps she liked it.

As for us, we set off to outrun the Kelpie home. It did not matter to Turkey, but she might lock me out again. I was almost in bed before I heard her come in. She went straight to her own room.

CHAPTER
THIRTY-ONE

A DOUBLE EXPOSURE

Whether the Kelpie had recognized us I could not tell, but not much of the next morning had passed before my doubt was over. When she had set our porridge on the table, she stood up, and with her fists to her sides, addressed my father.

"I'm very sorry, sir, to have to make complaints," she said. "It's a thing I don't like, and I'm not given to it. I'm sure I try to do my duty by Master Ranald as well as everyone else in this house."

I felt a little confused, for I now saw clearly enough that my father could not approve of our proceedings. I whispered to Allister.

"Run and fetch Turkey. Tell him to come directly."

Allister always did whatever I asked him. He set off at once. The Kelpie looked suspicious as he left the room, but she had no reason to interfere. I allowed her to tell the tale without interruption. After relating exactly how we had served her the night before when she had gone on a visit of mercy, as she represented it, she accused me of all my former tricks—that of the cat, I presume, enlightening her about the others. She ended by saying that if she were not protected against me and Turkey, she would have to leave the place.

"Let her go, Father," I said. "None of us like her."

"I like her," whimpered little Davie.

"Silence, sir!" said my father, very sternly. "Are these things true?"

"Yes, Father," I answered. "But please hear what *I've* got to say. She's only told you *her* side of it."

"You have confessed to the truth of what she said," said my father. "I did think," he went on, more in sorrow than in anger, though a good deal in both, "that you had turned from your mischievous ways. To think of my taking you with me to the deathbed of a holy man, and then finding you so soon after playing such tricks!—more like the mischievousness of a monkey than of a human being!"

"I don't say it was right, Father, and I'm very sorry if I have offended you."

"You *have* offended me, and very deeply. You have been unkind and indeed cruel to a good woman who has done her best for you for many years!"

I was not too much abashed to take notice that the Kelpie bridled at this.

"I can't say I'm sorry for what I've done to her," I said.

"Really, Ranald, you are impertinent. I would send you out of the room at once, but you must ask Mrs. Mitchell's forgiveness first, and after that there will be something more to say, I fear."

"But, Father, you have not heard my story yet."

"Well—go on. It is fair, I suppose, to hear both sides. But nothing can justify such conduct."

I began with a trembling voice. I had gone over in my mind the night before all I would say, knowing it was better to tell the tale from the beginning. Before I had ended, Turkey made his appearance, ushered in by Allister. Both were out of breath with running.

My father stopped me, and ordered Turkey away until I had finished. I ventured to look up at the Kelpie once or twice. She had grown white, and grew whiter. When Turkey left the room, she would have gone too. But my father told her she must stay and hear me out to the end. Several times she broke out, accusing me of telling a pack of wicked lies, but my father told her she should have an opportunity of defending herself, and she must not interrupt me.

When I was done, he called Turkey, and made him tell the story.

I need hardly say that, although he questioned us closely, he found no discrepancy between our accounts of what had happened. He turned at last to Mrs. Mitchell, who would have been in a sorry state by now if it had not been for her rage.

"Now, Mrs. Mitchell," he said.

She had nothing to reply beyond asserting that Turkey and I had always hated her and persecuted her, and had told a pack of lies which we had agreed upon, to ruin her, a poor lone woman, with no friends to take her side.

"I do not think it likely they could be so wicked," said my father.

"So, I'm to be the only wicked person in the world! Very well, sir. I will leave the house this very day!"

"No, no, Mrs. Mitchell. That won't do. One party or the other *is* wicked in this matter—that is clear. And it is of the greatest consequence to me to find out which. If you go, I shall know it is you, and I will have to have you taken up and tried for stealing. In the meantime, I shall go the round of the parish. I do not think all the poor people will have conspired to lie against you."

"They all hate me," said the Kelpie.

"And why?" asked my father.

She made no answer.

"I must get at the truth of it," said my father. "You can go now."

She left the room without another word, and my father turned to Turkey.

"I am surprised at you, Turkey, lending yourself to such silly pranks. Why did you not come and tell me?"

"I am very sorry, sir. I was afraid you would be troubled at finding what she was doing, and I thought we might frighten her away somehow. But Ranald began his tricks without letting me know, and then I saw that mine could be of no use, for she would suspect them after his. Mine would have been better, sir."

"I have no doubt of it, but equally unjustifiable. And you as well as he acted the part of a four-footed animal last night."

"I confess I yielded to temptation then, for I knew it could do no good. It was all for the pleasure of frightening her. It was a very foolish idea of mine, and I beg your pardon, sir."

"Well, Turkey, I confess you have angered me, not by trying to find out the wrong she was doing me and the whole parish, but by taking the whole thing into your own hands. It is worse of you, inasmuch as you are older and far wiser than Ranald. It is worse of Ranald, because I was his father."

He paused a moment, thinking, then continued to the two of us.

"I will try to show you the wrong you have done," he said. "Had you told me without doing anything yourselves, then I might have succeeded in bringing Mrs. Mitchell to repentance. I could have reasoned with her on the matter, and shown her that she was not merely a thief, but a thief of the worse kind, a Judas who robbed the poor, and so robbed God. I could have shown her how cruel she was—"

"Please, sir," interrupted Turkey. "I don't think, after all, that she did it for herself. I do believe," he went on, and my father listened, "that Wandering Willie is some relation of hers. He is the only poor person, almost the only person except Davie I ever saw her behave kindly to. He was there last night, and also, I have a feeling, on that other night when Ranald got such a fright. She has poor relations somewhere, and sends the meal to them by Willie. You remember, sir, there were no old clothes of Allister's to be found when you wanted them for Jamie Duff."

"You may be right, Turkey—I daresay you are right. I hope you are, for though bad enough, that would not be quite so bad as doing it for herself."

"I am very sorry, Father," I said. "Please forgive me."

"I hope it will be a lesson to you, my boy. After what you have done, rousing every bad and angry passion in her, I fear it will be of no use to try to make her be sorry and repent. It is to her, not to me, you have done the wrong. I have nothing to complain of for myself. Quite the contrary. But it is a very dreadful thing to throw difficulties in the way of repentance and turning from evil works."

"What can I do to make up for it?" I sobbed.

"I don't see at this moment what you can do. I will turn it over in my mind. You may go now."

Turkey and I walked away, I to school, he to his cattle. The lecture my father had given us was not to be forgotten. Turkey looked sad, and I felt subdued and concerned.

Everything my father heard confirmed the tale we had told him.

But the Kelpie frustrated whatever he may have resolved upon with regard to her. Before he returned she had disappeared. How she managed to get her chest away, I cannot tell. I think she must have hid it in one of the outbuildings, and fetched it the next night. Many little things were missed from the house, but nothing of great value, and neither she nor Wandering Willie ever appeared again. We were all satisfied that poor old Betty knew nothing of her conduct. It was easy enough to deceive her, for she was alone in her cottage, and only waited upon by a neighbor who visited her at certain times of the day.

I heard afterward that my father gave five shillings out of his own pocket to every one of the poor people whom the Kelpie had shortened of meal. Her place in the house was, to our endless happiness, taken by Kirsty, and faithfully she carried out my father's instructions that along with the sacred handful of meal, a penny should be given to every one of the parish poor from that time on, so long as he lived at the manse.

Not even little Davie cried when he found that Mrs. Mitchell was really gone. It was more his own affection than her kindness that had attached him to her.

Thus were we at last delivered from our Kelpie.

CHAPTER
THIRTY-TWO

—

BATTLE

A fter the expulsion of the Kelpie, and Kirsty's taking her place, things went on so peaceably, that the whole time rests in my memory like a summer evening after sundown. I have, therefore, little more to say concerning our home life.

There were two schools in the little town. The first was the parish school, whose schoolmaster was appointed by the presbytery. The second was supported by the dissenters who were not part of the Church of Scotland. Both, however, were licensed by the established church, and there were scholars in both schools whose fees were paid by the parish. Therefore, the distinction between the two schools was not actually that great. And my father was on friendly terms with all the parents, some of whom did not come to his church, and some who did. The only real schism in the matter was between the boys themselves, who made far more of the difference between the schools than their parents.

At this time there was at the second school a certain very rough lad. How it began I cannot recall, but this youth, a brute of seventeen, whether moved by dislike or the mere fascination of causing injury, was in the habit of teasing me beyond endurance as often as he had the chance. I did not like to complain to my father, though that would have been better than to hate him as I did. I was

169

ashamed of my own impotence to defend myself. But in that I was little to blame, for I was not more than half his size, and certainly not half his strength. Whenever we would meet in some out-of-the-way place, he would block my path for half an hour at least, pull my hair, pinch my cheeks, and do everything to annoy me, short of leaving marks of violence upon me. If we met in a street, or if other people were in sight, he would pass me with a wink and a grin, as much as to say—*Wait*.

One of the short but fierce wars between the rival schools broke out. What originated the individual quarrel I cannot tell. I doubt if anyone knew.

It had not lasted a day, however, before it came to a pitched battle after school hours. The second school was considerably smaller than ours, but it had the advantage of being perched on the top of the low, steep hill at the bottom of which lay ours.

Our battles always began with throwing whatever we could lay our hands on, and I wonder that so few serious accidents resulted. From the disadvantage of the ground, we had little chance against the stone showers, which came down upon us like hail unless we charged right up the hill in the face of the inferior but well-positioned enemy. When this was not being carried out, I busied myself in collecting stones and supplying them to my companions. It seemed that every boy—except me—down to the smallest in either school was skillful in throwing them. I could not throw halfway up the hill.

On this particular occasion, however, I began to fancy the gathering of stones an unworthy exercise of my fighting powers, and made my first attempt at organizing a troop for an uphill charge. I was now a rather tall boy and of some influence among those about my own age. Whether the enemy saw our intent and proceeded to forestall it, I cannot say. But certainly that charge never took place.

A house of some importance was then being built, just on the top of the hill. A sort of hand wagon on low wheels was in use for moving the large stones of the building. Our adversaries laid hold of this chariot and turned it into an engine of war. They dragged it to the top of the hill, jumped upon it, as many as it would hold, and drawn by their own weight, came thundering down upon our troops.

Vain was the storm of stones which we threw against their advance. They could not have stopped if they would. My company had to open and make way for the advancing wagon, conspicuous upon which towered my personal enemy Scroggie.

"Now," I called to my men, "as soon as the thing stops, rush in and seize them. They're not half our number. It will be an endless disgrace to let them go."

Whether we could have had the courage to carry out the design had not fortune favored us, I do not know. But as soon as the chariot reached a part of the hill where the slope was less, it turned a little to one side and Scroggie fell off, drawing half the load with him.

My men rushed in with shouts of defiant onset. But we were stopped almost instantly. I sprang to seize Scroggie. He tried to get up from where he lay on the ground, but fell back with a groan.

The moment I saw his face, my mood changed. My hatred, without will or wish or effort of mine, turned all at once into pity or something better. In a moment I was down on my knees beside him. His face was white, and drops stood on his forehead. He lay half upon his side, and was in obvious pain. His leg was broken.

I got him to lean his head against me, and tried to make him lie more comfortably. But the moment I sought to move the leg, he shrieked out. I sent one of our swiftest runners for the doctor, and in the meantime did the best I could for him. He took it as a matter of course and did not thank me. When the doctor came, we got a mattress from a neighboring house, laid it on the wagon, lifted Scroggie on the top, and dragged him up the hill and home to his mother.

CHAPTER
THIRTY-THREE

TRIBULATION

M y brother Tom had by now left the school and gone to the county town to receive some final preparation for the University. Consequently, so far as the school was concerned, I was no longer in the position of a younger brother.

Also, our master, Mr. Wilson, discovered that I had some ability to impart what knowledge I possessed, and had begun to make use of me in teaching some of the others.

The increasing trust the master placed in me gradually influenced my behavior to my schoolfellows in the form of vanity and presumption. And hence the complaint eventually arose that I was a favorite with the master, and the accusation that I used devious means to make myself look good in his eyes. I am not aware that I was actually guilty of this. But I do confess to the presumption, and wonder why the master did not take steps to correct it.

When teaching a class, if Mr. Wilson had left his chair, I would often climb into it and sit there as if I were the master of the school. I even went so far as to deposit some of my books in the master's desk instead of in my own little recess. But I had not the least suspicion of the indignation I was thus arousing against me.

One afternoon I had a class of history. They read very badly and seemed to be blundering on purpose. And when it came time for questioning on the subject of the lesson, I soon saw that there had been a conspiracy. The answers they gave were invariably wrong, generally absurd, sometimes utterly grotesque. I should say that most of the girls in the class did their best and apparently knew nothing of the design of the others. One or two girls, however, infected with the spirit of the game, soon outdid the whole class in the wildness of their replies.

This at last got the better of me. I lost my temper, threw down my book, and went to my seat, leaving the class where it stood.

The master called me and asked the reason. I told him the truth of the matter. He got very angry and called out several of the bigger boys and punished them severely. Whether they thought that I had mentioned them to him in particular, as I had not, I do not know. But I could read in their faces that they vowed vengeance in their hearts.

When the school broke up, I lingered to the last in hope that they would all go home as usual. But when I came out with the master, and saw the silent waiting groups, it was evident there was more thunder in the moral atmosphere that could be discharged without some lightning to go with it. The master had come to the same conclusion, for instead of turning toward his own house, he walked with me part of the way home, without saying a word about the reason. Allister was with us, and I led Davie by the hand. It was his first week of school life.

When we had got about half the distance, believing me now quite safe, he turned into a footpath and went through the fields back toward the town, while we jogged homeward.

When we had gone some distance farther, I happened to turn about. A crowd was following us at full speed. As soon as they saw that we had discovered them, they broke the silence with a shout, which was followed by the patter of many footsteps.

"Run, Allister!" I cried. I knelt down and caught up Davie on my back and ran with the feet of fear. Allister was soon far ahead of me.

"Bring Turkey!" I cried after him. "Run to the farm as fast as you can and bring Turkey to meet us."

Allister began running all the faster.

They were not catching up with us quite so fast as they wished.

They began to pick up stones as they ran, and we soon heard them hailing on the road behind us. A little farther and the stones began to go bounding past us, so that I dared no longer carry Davie on my back. I had to stop, which lost us time, and to shift him into my arms, which made running much harder.

Davie kept calling, "Run, Ranald!—here they come!" And with him jumping and twisting about in my arms, I found it very hard work indeed.

Their mocking voices at last began to reach me, loaded with all sorts of taunting words—some of them, I daresay, deserved, but not all. Next a stone struck me, but not in a dangerous place, though it crippled my running still more.

The bridge was now in sight, however, and there I could get rid of Davie and turn at bay. It was a small wooden bridge with rails and a narrow gate at the end to keep horsemen from riding over it. The closest of our pursuers were within a few yards of my heels, when, with a last effort, I bounded on it. I just had time to set Davie down and turn and bar their way by shutting the gate before they reached it.

I had no breath left, but just enough to cry, "Run, Davie!"

Davie, however, had no notion of the serious state of affairs. He did not run but stood behind me staring. So I was not much better off yet. If I had only seen him far enough on the way home, I would have taken to the water, which was here pretty deep. If I could have reached the mill on the opposite bank, a shout would have brought the miller to my aid. But so long as I could prevent them from opening the gate, I thought I could hold the position.

There was only a latch to secure it, but I pulled a thin knife from my pocket, and just as I received a blow in the face from the first arrival that knocked me backward, I had jammed it over the latch through the iron staple in which it worked. But they were soon attempting to remove the obstacle, though I disabled with a well-directed kick a few of the fingers that were fumbling with it. To protect the latch was now my main object, and in so doing I hardly saw the approach of my old adversary making his way through the ranks of the enemy.

They parted asunder, and Scroggie, still lame, strode heavily up to the gate. All I could think of was his old hatred of me. I turned once more and implored Davie, "Do run, Davie, dear! It's all up!" But my pleading was lost on him.

Turning again in despair, I saw the lame leg being hoisted up over the gate by twenty others. A shudder ran through me. I could *not* kick that leg. But I sprang up and hit Scroggie hard in the face. I might as well have hit a block of granite. He swore at me, caught hold of my hand, and turning to the rest of the evil troop, said:

"Now you be off! This is my little business! I do it for him!" Although they were far enough from obeying his orders, they were not willing to turn him into an enemy, so they hung back and watched. In the meantime the lame leg was by now on my side of the gate, the splits of which were sharpened at the points, and the sound leg was on the other. He had to let go of my hand in order to support himself, and I retreated a little, trembling. None of the rest of them could reach me as long as Scroggie was upon the top of the gate.

The lame leg went searching gently about, but could find no place to rest the sole of its foot, for there was no projecting crossbar on my side. The boards along the top were uneven, and the good leg suspended behind was useless too. The long and the short of it, both in legs and results, was that Scroggie had got himself temporarily stuck in his perch on top of the gate, and as long as he was stuck, I was safe.

As soon as I saw this, I turned and caught up Davie again, thinking to make for home once more. But that very instant there was a rush at the gate. Scroggie was hoisted over, the knife was taken out, and on poured the assailants before I had even reached the other end of the bridge.

"At them, Oscar!" cried a voice.

The dog rushed past me onto the bridge, followed by Turkey. I set Davie down, held on to his hand, and tried to catch my breath again. There was a scurry and a rush, a splash or two in the water, and then back came Oscar with his innocent tongue hanging out like a blood-red banner of victory. He was followed by Scroggie, who was exploding with laughter.

Oscar came up wagging his tail, and looking as pleased as if he had restored obedience to a flock of unruly sheep. I shrank back from Scroggie, wishing Turkey would hurry back from the other end of the bridge.

"Wasn't it fun, Ranald?" said Scroggie, still smiling.

I didn't understand his sudden friendliness! He saw my confusion.

"You don't think I was so lame that I couldn't get over that gate?" he said.

Still I stared at him bewildered.

"I stuck on purpose."

Turkey now joined us with a questioning look of his own, for he knew how Scroggie had been in the habit of treating me.

"It's all right, Turkey," I said, beginning to understand that my former foe had turned friend. "Scroggie stuck on the gate on purpose."

"A good thing for you, Ranald!" said Turkey. "Didn't you see Peter Mason among them?"

"No. He left the school last year."

"He was there though, and I don't suppose *he* meant to be agreeable."

"I tell you what," said Scroggie. "If you like, I'll leave my school and come to yours. My mother lets me do as I like."

I thanked him, but said I did not think there would be more of it. It would blow over.

Allister told my father as much as he knew of the affair. And when he questioned me, I told him as much as I knew.

The next morning, just as we were all settling into our work, my father entered the school. The hush that followed was intense. The place might have been absolutely empty judging from any sound I could hear. The ringleaders of my enemies held down their heads, anticipating an outbreak of vengeance.

But after a few moments conversation with Mr. Wilson, my father departed. There was a mystery about the proceeding, an unknown possibility of result. It had a very calming effect upon the whole morning.

When we broke up for dinner, Mr. Wilson detained me, and told me that my father thought it better that, for some time at least, I should not occupy such a prominent position as before. He was very sorry, he said, for I had been a great help to him. And if I did not object, he would ask my father to allow me to assist him in the evening school during the winter. I was delighted at the idea, sank back into my natural position among my classmates, and met with no more annoyance. After a while I was able to assure my former foes that I had not singled them out for punishment, and thus the hard feelings were quite extinguished.

There were a few girls at the evening school as well—among the rest, Elsie Duff.

Although her grandmother was very feeble, Elsie was now able to have a little more of her own way, and there was no reason why the old woman should not be left for an hour or two in the evening. I need hardly say that Turkey was also a regular attendant in the evenings. He always, and I sometimes, saw Elsie home.

My chief pleasure lay in helping her with her lessons. I did my best to assist all who wanted my aid, but no doubt offered her the most attention of all. She was not quick, but would never be satisfied until she understood something, and that is more than any superiority of gifts. Hence, if her progress was slow, it was steady. Turkey was far ahead of me in trigonometry, but I was able to help him in grammar and geography. And when he began Latin, which he did the same winter, I assisted him a good deal.

Sometimes Mr. Wilson would ask me to go home with him after school and have supper with him. This made me late, but my father did not mind it, for he liked me to be with Mr. Wilson. I learned a good deal from him at such times. He had an excellent little library, and would take down his favorite books and read me passages.

It is wonderful how things, which in reading for ourselves we might pass over half-blind, gain their true power and influence through the voice of one who sees and feels what is in them. If a man in whom you have confidence merely lays his finger on a paragraph and says to you, "Read that," you will probably discover three times as much in it as you would if you had only chanced upon it in the course of your reading. In such an instance, the mind gathers itself up and is all eyes and ears.

But Mr. Wilson would sometimes read me a few verses of his own. And this was a delight such as I had rarely experienced. You may wonder why a full-grown man and a good scholar would treat a boy like me as so much of an equal. But sympathy of heart and mind is precious, even from a child, and Mr. Wilson had no companions of his own standing. I think he read even more to Turkey than to me, however.

As I have once apologized for the introduction of a few of his verses with Scotch words in them, I will hope that the same apology will cover a second offense of the same sort.

JEANIE BRAW[1]

I like ye weel upo' Sundays, Jeanie,
In yer goon an' yer ribbons gay;
But I like ye better on Mondays, Jeanie,
And I like ye better the day[2].

For it will come into my heid, Jeanie,
O' yer braws[3] ye are thinkin' a wee;
No' a' o' the Bible-seed, Jeanie,
Nor the minister nor me.

And hame across the green, Jeanie,
Ye gang wi' a toss o'yer chin:
Us twa there's a shadow atween, Jeanie,
Though yer hand my airm lies in.

But noo, whan I see ye gang, Jeanie,
Busy wi' what's to be dune,
Liltin' a haveless[4] sang, Jeanie,
I could kiss yer verra shune.
Wi' yer silken net on yer hair, Jeanie,
In yer bonny blue petticoat,

Wi' yer kindly arms a' bare, Jeanie,
On yer verra shadow I doat.
For oh! but ye're eident[5] and free, Jeanie,
Airy o' hert and o' fit[6];
There's a licht shines oot o'yer ee, Jeanie;
O' yersel' ye thinkna a bit.

Turnin' or steppin' alang, Jeanie,

---

[1]Brave; well dressed
[2]Today
[3]Bravery; finery
[4]Careless
[5]Diligent
[6]Foot

TRIBULATION

Liftin' an' layin' doon,
Settin' richt what's aye gaein' wrang, Jeanie,

Yer motion's baith dance an' tune.
Fillin' the cogue fra the coo, Jeanie,
Skimmin' the yallow cream,
Poorin' awa' the het broo, Jeanie,
Lichtin' the lampie's leme[7]—

I' the hoose ye're a licht an' a law, Jeanie,
A servant like him that's abune:
Oh! a woman's bonniest o' a', Jeanie,
Whan she's doin' what maun be dune.

Sae, dressed in yer Sunday claes, Jeanie,
Fair kythe ye amang the fair;
But dressed in yer ilka-days,[9] Jeanie,
Yer beauty's beyond compare.

---

[7]Flame
[8]Appear
[9]Everyday clothes

A WINTER'S RIDE

This winter was the stormiest I can ever remember. During it the chief adventure of my boyhood occurred—indeed, the event most worthy to be called an adventure I have ever encountered.

There had been a tremendous snowfall. A furious wind, lasting two days and a night, had drifted the snow up into great mounds, so that the shape of the country was completely changed with new heights and hollows. Even those who were best acquainted with them could only guess at the direction of some of the roads, and it was the easiest thing in the world to lose the right track, even in broad daylight.

As soon as the storm was over, however, and the freezing frost was found likely to continue, people had begun to cut passages through some of the deeper snow mounds. And over the tops of others, and along the general line of the busier roads, footpaths had soon been made. But it was many days before vehicles could pass and coaches could again run between the towns.

All the short day the sun was low and brilliant, and the whole country shone with dazzling whiteness. But after sunset, which took place between three and four o'clock, a more dreary place could hardly be imagined, especially when the keenest of winds rushed in gusts from the northeast, lifted the snow powder from shadows, and blew it like a thousand stings in the face of a freezing traveler.

Early one afternoon, just as I came home from school, which in winter was always over at three o'clock, my father received a message that a certain laird, or squire as he would be called in England—whose house lay three or four miles off among the hills—was at the point of death and very anxious to see him. A groom on horseback had brought the message. The old man had led not the best of lives, and that probably made him all the more anxious to see my father, who proceeded at once to get ready for the uninviting journey.

Since my brother Tom's departure for the University, I had become yet more of a companion to my father. When I now saw him preparing to set out, I asked if I could go with him. His little black mare had a daughter. She was almost twice her mother's size, but so clumsy she was used mostly about the farm. She had a touch of the roadster in her, and if not quite capable of elegant motion, could get over the ground well enough, with a sort of speedy slouch. She was also of great strength, which was most important on an expedition like the present.

My father hesitated, looked out at the sky, and replied, "I hardly know what to say, Ranald. If I were sure of the weather—but I am very doubtful. However, if it should break up, we can stay there all night. Yes.—Here, Allister, run and tell Andrew to saddle both the mares and bring them down directly.—Make haste with your dinner, Ranald."

Delighted at the prospect, I did make haste. The meal was soon over, and Kirsty took great care in clothing me for the journey, which would certainly be much longer in time than in actual distance. In half an hour we were all mounted and on our way—the groom, who had just come with the message, a few yards in front of my father and me.

I have already said that my father took comparatively little notice of us children, beyond what teaching he gave us and the nightly family prayers. He rarely touched us, or did anything to try to make up in that way the loss of our mother. I believe his thoughts were tenderness itself toward us, but they did not show themselves in the shape of tender gestures.

It seems to me now that perhaps he was wisely retentive of his feelings, and waited for a better time to let them flow. For always as we grew older, we drew nearer to my father, or more properly, he drew nearer to us. Gradually he dropped that reticence which perhaps too many parents keep up until their children are full-grown.

Thus, by this time he was in the habit of conversing with me most freely. I presume he had found, or believed he had found me trustworthy not to repeat any remarks he might make. But much as he hated certain kinds of gossip, he believed that indifference to your neighbor and his affairs was worse. He said everything depended on the spirit in which men spoke of each other. He said that much of what was called gossip was only a natural love of biography, and if it was kindly, there was little wrong in it. The greater part of gossip was wrong, he said, because it stemmed from curiosity, not love. But worst of all, which he called among the wickedest things on earth, was that talk about people that had as its chief object the desire to believe, and make others believe, the worst concerning someone. I mention these opinions of my father so that you will understand his talking to me as he did.

Our horses made very slow progress. It was almost nowhere possible to trot. We had to plod on, step by step. This made it easier to talk.

"This country looks dreary, doesn't it, Ranald?" he said.

"Just like as if everything were dead, Father," I replied.

"If the sun were to stop shining altogether, what do you think would happen?"

I thought a bit, but was not prepared to answer when my father spoke again.

"What makes the seeds grow, Ranald—the oats and the wheat and the barley?"

"The rain, Father," I said, with half knowledge.

"Well, if there were no sun, the vapors would not rise to make clouds. What rain there was already in the sky would come down in snow or lumps of ice. The earth would grow colder and colder, and harder and harder, until at last it went sweeping through the air, one frozen mass, as hard as stone, without a green leaf or a living creature upon it."

"How dreadful to think of, Father!" I said. "That would be frightful!"

"Yes, my boy. It is the sun that is the life of the world. Not only does he make the rain rise to fall on the seeds in the earth, but even that would be useless if he did not make them warm as well—and do something else to them besides which we cannot understand."

"What else does the sun do?" I asked.

"Farther down into the earth than any of the rays of his light can reach, he sends other rays we cannot see, which go searching about in it, like long fingers. And wherever they find and touch a seed, the life that is in that seed begins to talk to itself, as it were, and immediately begins to grow."

"Does the sun really do that?"

My father smiled. "He makes it happen," he said. "Out of the dark earth he brings all the lovely green things of the spring, and clothes the world with beauty, and sets the waters running, and the birds singing, and the lambs bleating, and the children gathering daisies and buttercups, and the gladness overflowing in all their hearts."

He paused a moment, then said, "That is all very different from what we see now—isn't it, Ranald?"

"Yes, Father. It is hard to believe, to look at it now, that the world will ever be like that again."

"But for as cold and wretched as it looks, the sun has not forsaken it. He has only drawn away from it for a little, for good reasons, one of which is that we may learn that we cannot do without him. If he were to go, we could not draw one more breath. Horses and men would drop down into frozen lumps, as hard as stones."

He paused again. "Who is the sun's father, Ranald?" he asked at length.

"He hasn't got a father," I replied, hoping for some answer to a riddle.

"Yes he has, Ranald. I can prove it. You remember whom the apostle James calls the Father of Lights?"

"Of course, Father. But doesn't that mean another kind of lights?"

"Yes. But they couldn't be called lights if they were not like the sun. All kinds of lights must come from the Father of Lights. Now the Father of the sun must be like the sun, and indeed of all material things, the sun is the most like God. We pray to God to shine upon us and give us light. If God did not shine into our hearts, they would be dead lumps of cold. We wouldn't care for anything whatever."

"Then God never stops shining upon us. He wouldn't be like the sun if he did. For even in the winter the sun shines enough to keep us alive."

"True, my boy. I am very glad you understand me. In all my experience I have never yet known a man in whose heart I could not find proofs of the shining of the great Sun. It might be a very feeble wintry shine, but he was still there. For a human heart though, it is very dreadful to have a cold, white winter like this inside it, instead of a summer of color and warmth and light. Take the man we're going to see, for instance. They talk of the winter of age. That's all very well, but the heart is not made for winter. A man may have the snow on his roof and merry children about his hearth. He may have gray hairs on his head and the very gladness of summer in his heart. But this old man, I am afraid, feels wintry cold within."

"Then why doesn't the Father of Lights shine more on him and make him warmer?"

"The sun is shining as much on the earth in the winter as in the summer. So why do you suppose the earth is no warmer?"

"Because," I answered, calling up what little astronomy I knew, "that part of it is turned away from the sun."

"Just so. Then if a man turns himself away from the Father of Lights—the great Sun—how can he be warmed?"

"But the earth can't help it, Father."

"But the man can, Ranald. He feels the cold, and he knows he can turn to the light. Even this poor old man knows it now. God is shining on him—a wintry way—or he would not feel the cold at all. He would only be a lump of ice, a part of the very winter itself. The good of what warmth God gives him is that he feels the cold. If he were all cold, he couldn't feel cold."

"Does he want to turn to the Sun?"

"I don't know. I only know that he is miserable because he has not turned to the Sun."

"What will you say to him, Father?"

"I cannot tell, my boy. It depends on what I find him thinking. Of all things, my boy, keep your face to the Sun. You can't shine by yourself, you can't be good by yourself, but God has made you able to turn to the Sun from which all goodness and all shining comes. God's children may be very naughty, but they must be able to turn toward him. The Father of Lights is the Father of every weakest little baby of a good thought in us, as well as of the highest devotion of servanthood, even martyrdom. If you turn your face to the Sun, my boy, your soul will, when you come to die, feel like an autumn, with the golden fruits of the earth hanging in rich clusters ready to be gathered—not like a winter. You may feel ever so worn, but you will not feel withered. You will die in peace, hoping for the spring—and such a spring!"

Thus talking, in the course of two hours or so we arrived at the dwelling of the old laird.

Chapter Thirty-five

THE OLD LAIRD

How dreary the old house looked as we approached it in the gathering darkness! All the light appeared to come from the snow which rested wherever it could lie—on roofs and window ledges and turrets. Even on the walls, the roughness held little frozen patches, so that the gray of the stone was spotted all over with whiteness. Not a glimmer of light shone from the windows.

"Surely nobody lives *there*, Father," I said.

"It does not look very lively," he answered.

The house stood on a bare knoll. There was not a tree within sight. Rugged hills arose on all sides of it. Not a sound was heard but the moan of an occasional gust of wind. There was a brook, but it lay frozen beneath yards of snow. For miles in any direction those gusts might wander without shaking door or window.

We were crossing the yard at the back of the house, toward the kitchen door, for the front door had not been opened for months, when we recognized the first sign of life. That was only the low of a calf. As we dismounted on a few feet of rough pavement which had been swept clear, an old woman came to the door and led us into a dreary parlor without even a fire in it to welcome us.

I learned afterward that the laird, from being a spendthrift in his youth, had become a miser in his old age. So everything about the household was pinched in the narrowest possible way.

After we had remained standing for some time, the housekeeper returned and invited my father to go to the laird's room. As they went, he asked her to take me to the kitchen. She did so the moment she returned from conducting him. The sight of the fire, although it was small, was certainly welcome. She laid a few more peats on it, encouraged them to a blaze, and then remarked, "We wouldn't dare do this if the laird was up and about, you see, sir. He would call it a waste."

"Is he dying?" I asked, for the sake of saying something. But she only shook her head in reply. Then, going to a cupboard at the other end of the large kitchen, she brought me some milk in a bowl, and some oatcake on a plate.

"It's not my house, you see," she said, "or I would have something better to set before the minister's son."

I was glad for any food, however, and it was well for me that I ate heartily. I had got quite warm also before my father stepped into the kitchen, very solemn, and stood with his back to the fire. The old woman set him a chair, but he neither sat down nor accepted the food she humbly offered him.

"We must be going," he said, "for it looks stormy, and the sooner we set out the better."

"I'm sorry I can't ask you to stay the night," she said, "but I would not be able to make you comfortable. There's nothing fit to offer you in the house, and there's not a bed that's been slept in for I don't know how long."

"Never mind," said my father cheerfully. "The moon is up already, and we shall get home I trust before the snow begins to fall. Will you tell the man to get our horses out?"

When she returned from taking the message, she came up to my father and spoke in a loud whisper.

"Is he in a bad way, sir?"

"He is dying," answered my father.

"I know that," she returned. "He'll be gone before the morning. But that's not what I meant. Is he in a bad way for the other world? That's what I meant, sir."

"Well, my good woman, after a life like his, we are only too glad to remember what our Lord told us—not to judge. I do think he is ashamed and sorry for his past life. But it's not the wrong he has done in former times that stands half so much in his way as his present love for what he counts his own. It seems about to break his heart to leave all the little bits of property—particularly the money he has saved. And yet he has some hope that Jesus Christ will be kind enough to pardon him. I am afraid he will find himself very miserable though, when he has not one scrap left to call his own—not even a pocketknife."

"It's dreadful to think of him flying through the air on a night like this," she said.

"My good woman," returned my father, "we know nothing about where or how the departed spirit exists after it leaves the body. But it seems to me just as dreadful to be without God in the world as to be without him anywhere else. Let us pray for him that God may be with him wherever he is."

So saying, my father knelt down, and we beside him, and he prayed earnestly to God for the old man. Then we rose, mounted our horses, and rode away.

CHAPTER
THIRTY-SIX
—

THE PEAT STACK

We were only about halfway home when the clouds began to cover the moon, and the snow began to fall.

We had got on pretty well till then, for there was light enough to see the track, as weak as it was. Now, however, we had to keep a careful look. We pressed our horses, and they went bravely, but it was slow work at best.

It got darker and darker, for the clouds went on gathering, and the snow was coming down in huge dull flakes. Faster and thicker they came, until at length we could see nothing of the road in front of us, and were forced to leave all to the wisdom of our horses. My father had great confidence in his own little mare, who had carried him through many a doubtful and difficult place, and rode first. I followed close behind. He kept on talking to me very cheerfully to prevent me from getting frightened.

But I had not a thought of fear. To be with my father was to me perfect safety. He was in the act of telling me how, on more occasions than one, Missy had got him through places where the road was impassable, by walking on the tops of the walls, when all at once both our horses plunged into a gulf of snow. The more my mare struggled, the deeper we sank in it. For a moment I thought it was closing over my head.

190

"Father! Father!" I shouted.

"Don't be frightened, my boy!" cried my father, his voice seeming to come from far away. "We are in God's hands. I can't help you now, but as soon as Missy has got quieter, I shall come to you. I think I know whereabouts we are. We've dropped right off the road. You're not hurt, are you?"

"Not in the least," I answered. "I was only frightened."

A few seconds more and my mare lay stuck in the snow nearly motionless, with her head thrown back and her body deep in the drift. I put up my hands to feel. The snow rose above my head farther than I could reach. I got clear of the stirrups and scrambled up, first on my knees, and then on my feet. Now I was standing on top of the saddle. Again I stretched my hands above my head, but still the broken wall of snow was taller above me than I could reach. I could see nothing of my father, but heard him talking to Missy.

My mare soon began floundering again, so that I tumbled about against the sides of the hole, and grew terrified that I might bring the snow down on top of me. I therefore knelt down on the mare's back until she was quiet again.

"Whoa! Quiet, my lass!" I heard my father saying, and it seemed his Missy was more frightened than mine.

My fear was by now quite gone, and I almost felt like laughing at the fun of the adventure. I had yet no idea of how serious a thing it might be. Still I had sense enough to see that something must be done. But what? I saw no way of getting out of the hole except by trampling down the snow upon the back of my poor mare, and I doubted very much if my father could even tell in what direction we should turn for help or shelter. It seemed out of the question that we would be able to find our way home, even if we did get out of the snow hole.

Again my mare began plunging about violently, and this time I found myself thrown against some hard substance. I thrust my hand through the snow and found what I thought were the stones of one of the dry walls common to the country. I might be able to clear away enough of the snow to climb upon it. But then what next?—it was so dark.

"Ranald!" cried my father. "How are you getting on?"

"Much the same, Father," I answered.

"I'm out of the hole," he returned. "We've come through on the other side. You are better where you are I suspect, however. The snow is warmer than the air. It is beginning to blow. Pull your feet out and get right upon the mare's back."

"That's just where I am, Father—lying on her back, and pretty comfortable," I answered.

All this time the snow was falling thick. If it went on like this, I would be buried before morning, and the fact that the wind was rising added to the danger of it. We were at the wrong end of the night too.

"I'm in a kind of ditch, I think, Father," I cried," between the place we fell off on one side and a stone wall on the other."

"That can hardly be, or I shouldn't have got out," he returned. "But now that I've got Missy quiet, I'll come to you. I must get you out, I see, or you will be snowed in. Whoa, Missy! Good mare! Stand still."

The next moment he gave a joyous exclamation. "What is it, Father?" I cried.

"It's not a stone wall—it's a peat stack. That *is* good."

"I don't see what good it is. We can't light a fire."

"No, my boy. But where there's a peat stack[1], there's probably a house."

He began a series of shouts at the top of his voice, listening in between for a response. This lasted a good while. I began to get very cold.

"I'm nearly frozen, Father," I said, "and what's to become of the poor mare—she's got no clothes on?"

"I'll get you out, my boy. And then you will at least be able to move about a little."

I heard him shoveling at the snow with his hands and feet.

"I have got to the corner of the stack, and as well as I can judge,

---

[1]*Peats* are small brick-sized blocks of dried root-mass used in Scotland as fuel for fire and the chief source of winter warmth. They are cut from surrounding fields and moors, dried, and then piled in great stacks for use throughout the winter, in just the same way as a woodpile would be in areas where trees are plentiful.

you must be just around the other side of it," he called through the snow.

"Your voice is getting closer," I answered.

"I've got hold of one of the mare's ears," he said next. "I won't try to get her out until I get you off her."

I put out my hand, and felt along the mare's neck. What a joy it was to catch my father's hand through the darkness and the snow! He grasped mine and drew me toward him, then got me by the arm and began dragging me through the snow. The mare began plunging again, and by her struggles rather assisted my father. In a few moments he had me in his arms.

"Thank God!" he said as he set me down against the peat stack. "Stand there. A little farther. Keep well away or she could hurt you. She must fight her way out now."

He went back to the mare and went on clearing away the snow. Then I could hear him patting and encouraging her. Next I heard a great blowing and scrambling, and at last a snort and thunder of hoofs.

"Whoa! whoa! Gently! gently!—She's off!" cried my father.

Her mother gave one snort, and away she went, thundering after her. But their sounds were soon quenched in the snow.

"There's a business!" said my father. "I'm afraid the poor things will only go farther to wind up faring the worse. We are as well without them, however. And if they should find their way home, so much the better for us. They might have kept us a little warmer though. We must fight the cold as best we can for the rest of the night. It would be folly to leave this spot before it is light enough to see where we are going."

It came into my mind suddenly how I had burrowed in the straw to hide myself after running from Dame Shand's. But whether that or the thought of burrowing in the peat stack came first, I cannot tell. I turned to feel whether I could draw out a peat. With a little loosening I succeeded.

"We could make a hole in the peat stack, Father," I said, "and build ourselves in."

"A capital idea, my boy!" he answered, with gladness in his voice. "We'll try it at once."

"I've got two or three out already," I said, for I had gone on pulling, and it was easy enough after one had been started.

"We must take care we don't bring down the whole stack though," said my father. "Here," he added, "I will put my stick in under the top row. That will be a sort of lintel to support those above."

He always carried his walking stick whether he rode or walked.

We worked with a will, piling up the peats a little in front so that we might build up the door of our cave after we were inside. We got quite merry in the process of our work.

"We shall be brought before the magistrates for destruction of property," said my father.

"You'll have to send Andrew to build up the stack again—that's all."

"But I wonder why nobody is able to hear us. How can they have a peat stack so far from the house?"

"I can't imagine," I said, "except it be to prevent them from burning too many peats. It is more like a trick of the poor than anybody else."

Every now and then a few peats would fall down with a rush, and before long we had made a large hole. We left a good thick floor to sit upon.

Creeping in, we began building up the entrance behind us. We had not proceeded far, however, before we found that our cave was too small, and that we would find it very cramped since we would have to remain in it for hours. Therefore, instead of using any more of the peats already pulled out, we finished building up the wall with others fresh drawn from the inside.

When at length we had, to the best of our ability, completed enclosing ourselves, we sat down to wait for the morning—my father as calm as if he had been seated in his study chair, and I in a state of condensed delight. For was this not a grand adventure—with my father to share it and keep it from going too far? I was utterly unconscious of the potential direfulness of our circumstances.

My father sat with his back against the side of the hole, and I sat between his knees and leaned against him. His arms were folded round me, and could ever a boy be more blessed than I was then? The sense of outside danger, the knowledge that if the wind rose, we might be walled up in snow before morning, the assurance of present safety and good hope—all made such an impression upon my mind that ever since when any trouble has threatened me, I have invariably turned first in thought to the memory of that harbor of refuge from the storm.

There I sat for long hours secure in my father's arms. I knew that the soundless snow was falling thick around us. The silence was marked occasionally by the threatening wail of the wind like the cry of a wild beast scenting us from afar.

"This is grand, Father," I said.

"You would like better to be at home in bed, wouldn't you?" he asked.

"No, indeed," I answered with complete honesty, for I felt exuberantly happy.

"If only we can keep warm," said my father. "If you should get very cold indeed, you must not lose heart, my man. Just think how pleasant it will be when we get home to a good fire and a hot breakfast."

"I think I can bear it all right. I have often been cold at school."

"This may be worse. But we need not anticipate evil. That is to send out for the suffering. It is well to be prepared for it, but it is not good to brood over an imagined future of evil. In all my life, my boy—and I want you to remember what I say—I have never found any trial go beyond what I could bear. In the worst case of suffering, I think there is help given which those who look on from the outside cannot understand, but which enables the sufferer to endure. The last help of that kind is death, which I think is always a blessing, though few people can regard it as such."

I listened with some wonder. Without being able to see that what he said was true, I could yet accept it after a vague fashion.

"This nest we have made to shelter us," he resumed, "reminds me of what the psalmist says about dwelling in the secret place of the Most High. Everyone who will may there, like the swallow, make himself a nest."

"But surely this can't be very much like that, can it, Father?" I ventured to object.

"Why not, my boy?"

"It's not safe enough, for one thing."

"You are right there. Still it is like it in a way. It is our place of refuge, however incomplete."

"But the cold does get through."

"But it keeps our minds at peace. Even the refuge in God does not always secure us from external suffering. The heart may be quite happy and strong when the hands are benumbed with cold. Yes, the heart may even grow cold with coming death, while the man himself retreats all the further into the secret place of the Most High, growing more calm and hopeful as the last cold invades the house of his body. I believe that all troubles come to drive us into that refuge—that secret place where alone we can be safe. You will, when you get older and go out into the world, find that most men not only do not believe this, but do not believe that you believe it. They regard it at best as a fantastic weakness, fit only for weak or sickly or elderly people.

"But watch how the strength of such people and their calmness and common sense fares when the grasp of suffering lays hold upon them. It was a sad sight—that hopeless misery I saw this afternoon. If the laird's mind had been an indication of the reality, you would have to say that there was no God—no God at least that would have anything to do with him. The universe as reflected in the tarnished mirror of his soul was a chill misty void of emptiness through which blew the moaning wind of an unknown fate. As near as I ever saw it, that man was without God and without a single hope in the world.

"All those who have done the mightiest things throughout history—and I do not mean the showiest things; I'm not talking about the most *famous* of men, but the *mightiest*—all these, I say, who have done the mightiest things and been the mightiest sort of men on the inside, have not only believed that there was this refuge in God, but have themselves more or less entered into the secret place of the Most High. There only could they have found strength to do their mighty deeds, and to become the mighty men they were. They were able to do them because they knew God wanted them to do them, knew that he was on their side, or rather that they were on his side, and therefore safe, surrounded by God on every side. My boy, do the will of God—that is, what you know or believe to be right, and fear nothing."

I never forgot the lesson. And what circumstances in which to be taught it! You must not think that my father often talked like this. He was not inclined to a great deal of talk about spiritual things. He preferred to let his life speak for him. He used to say that much talk prevented much thought, and talk without thought was bad.

Therefore, it was for the most part only upon extraordinary occasions, of which this is an example, that he spoke of the deep simplicities of that faith in God which was the very root of his conscious life.

He was silent after this speech, which lasted longer than I have represented. It was unbroken, I believe, by any remark of mine.

Full of inward peace, I fell asleep in his arms.

Chapter Thirty-seven

AN UNEXPECTED
VISITOR

W hen I awoke I found myself very cold.

Then I became aware that my father was asleep. For the first time I began to be uneasy.

It was not because of the cold. I could endure that. It was that while the night lay awful in white silence about me, while the wind was moaning outside and blowing long thin currents through the peat walls around me, while our warm home lay far away, and I could not tell how many hours of cold darkness had yet to pass before we could set out to find it—it was not all these things together that began to make me anxious. It was that in the midst of all these, I was awake and my father slept.

I could easily have waked him, but I was not so selfish as that. So I sat still and shivered and felt very dreary, and have to confess now and then was a little afraid.

Then the last words of my father began to return to me. And with a throb of relief, the thought awoke in my mind that, although my father was asleep, the great Father of us both, in whose heart lay that secret place of refuge, neither slumbered nor slept. And now I was able to wait in patience, with an idea, if not a sense of the present care of God, such as I had never had before. When, after some years, my father was taken from us, the thought of this night came again and again to me, and I would say in my heart, "My father sleeps that I may the better know that the Father wakes."

At length he stirred. The first sign of his awaking was that he closed again the arms about me which had dropped by his sides as he slept.

"I'm so glad you're awake, Father," I said, speaking first.

"Have *you* been awake long, then?" he asked.

"Not so very long, but I felt lonely without you."

"Are you very cold?"

"Yes, rather."

"I am rather chilly too."

So we chatted away for a while.

"I wonder if it is nearly day yet. I have no idea how long we slept."

"It seems like hours and hours," I said.

"I wonder if my watch is going. I forgot to wind it up last night. If it has stopped, I shall know it is nearly daylight."

He held his watch to his ear. Alas! it was ticking vigorously. He felt for the keyhole, and wound the watch. After that we busied ourselves in repeating as many of the psalms and paraphrases of Scripture as we could remember, and this helped to while away a good part of the weary time.

But it went slowly, and I was growing so cold that I could hardly bear it. "I'm afraid you feel very cold, Ranald," said my father, folding me closer in his arms. "You must try not to go to sleep again, for that would be dangerous now. I feel more cramped than cold."

As he said this, he extended his legs and threw his head back to get rid of the discomfort by stretching himself. The same moment, down came a shower of peats upon our heads and bodies. When I tried to move I found myself stuck. I could not help laughing.

"Father," I cried as soon as I could speak, "you're like Samson. You've brought the house down upon us!"

"So I have, my boy. It was very thoughtless of me. I don't know what we are to do now."

"Can you move, Father? *I* can't," I said.

"I can move my legs, but I'm afraid to even move a toe in my boot for fear of bringing down another avalanche of peats. But no—there's not much danger of that—they are all down already. I feel the snow on my face."

With hands and feet my father struggled, but could not do much, for I lay against him under a great heap. His struggles did make an opening sideways, however.

"Father! Father!" I cried, "shout out! I see a light somewhere, and I think it is moving!"

We shouted as loud as we could, and then lay listening. My heart beat so loud I was afraid I would not hear any reply that might come. But the next moment it rang through the frosty air.

"It's Turkey! That's Turkey, Father!" I cried. "I know his shout. He can make it go further than anybody else.—Turkey! Turkey!" I shrieked, almost weeping with delight.

Again Turkey's cry rang through the darkness, and the wavering light drew nearer.

"Watch how you step, Turkey!" cried my father. There's a hole you may tumble into."

"It wouldn't hurt him much in the snow," I said.

"Perhaps not, but he would probably lose his light, and that we can hardly afford."

"Shout again," cried Turkey. "I can't make out where you are." My father shouted.

"Am I coming nearer to you now?"

"I can hardly say. I cannot see well. Are you going along the road?"

"Yes. Can't you come to me?"

"Not yet. We can't get out. We're on your right, stuck in a peat stack."

"Oh, I know the stack! I'll be with you in a moment."

He did not, however, find it so easily as he had expected since the peats were completely buried in snow. My father gave up trying to free himself, and took to laughing instead at the ridiculous situation we were about to be discovered in. He kept shouting out directions to Turkey, who at length after some disappearances, which made us very anxious about the lantern, caught sight of the stack and walked straight toward it. Now for the first time we saw that he was not alone, but accompanied by the silent Andrew.

"Where are you, sir?" asked Turkey, throwing the light of the lantern over the ruin.

"Buried in the peats," answered my father, laughing. "Come and get us out."

Turkey strode up to the heap and turned the light down into it. "I didn't know it had been raining peats, sir," he said.

"The peats didn't fall quite so far as the snow, Turkey, or they would have made a worse job of it," answered my father.

In the meantime, Turkey and Andrew were both busy, and in a few moments we stood upon our feet, stiff with cold, cramped with confinement, but merry enough at heart.

"What brought you out to look for us?" asked my father.

"I heard Missy whinnying at the stable door," said Andrew. "When I saw she was alone, I knew something had happened, and woke Turkey. We only stopped to run to the manse for a drop of whiskey to bring with us, and then we set out at once."

"What time is it?" asked my father.

"About one o'clock," answered Andrew.

One o'clock! I thought. *What a time we would have had to wait!*

"Have you been long in finding us?"

"Only about an hour."

"Then the little mare must have had great trouble in getting home. You say the other was not with her?"

"No, sir. She's made no appearance."

"Then if we don't find her, she will be dead before morning. But what shall we do with you, Ranald? Turkey had better go home with you first."

"Please let me go with you," I said.

"Are you able to walk?"

"Quite—or at least I shall be after my legs come a bit more to themselves."

Turkey produced a bottle of milk, which he had brought for me, and Andrew produced the little flask of whiskey that Kirsty had sent. My father took a little of the latter, while I emptied my bottle.

Then we set out to look for young Missy.

"Where are we?" asked my father.

Turkey told him.

"How is it that nobody heard our shouting, then?"

"You know, sir," answered Turkey, "the old man is as deaf as a post, and I daresay all his people were fast asleep."

The snow was falling only in a few large flakes now, which sank through the air like the descending of tiny lovely birds of heaven. The moon had come out again, and the white world lay around us in lovely light. A good deal of snow had fallen while we lay in the peats, but we could yet trace the track of the two horses. We followed it a long way through the little valley into which we had dropped from the side of the road.

We came to more places than one where the mares had been floundering together in piles of snow, but at length we reached a spot where one had parted from the other. When we had traced one of the tracks to the road, we concluded it was Missy's, and returned to the other. We had not followed it very far before we came upon the poor mare lying upon her back in a deep pit, in which the snow was very soft. She had put her forefeet in it as she galloped heedlessly along, and tumbled right over. The snow had yielded enough to let the banks get ahold of her, and she lay helpless.

Turkey and Andrew had brought spades with them and a rope, and they set to work at once, my father taking a turn now and then, and I holding the lantern, which was all but useless now in the moonlight. It took more than an hour to get the poor thing on her legs again. But when she was up, it was all they could do to hold her. She was so wild with cold and with delight at feeling her legs under her once more that she would have broken loose again and galloped off as recklessly as ever.

They set me on her back, and with my father on one side and Turkey on the other, and Andrew at her head, I rode home in great comfort. It was another good hour before we arrived, and right glad were we to see through the curtains of the parlor the glow of the great fire which Kirsty had kept up for us.

She burst out crying when we made our appearance.

Chapter Thirty-eight

A SOLITARY CHAPTER

During all that winter I attended the evening school and assisted the schoolmaster.

When school was over, Turkey and I walked home with Elsie Duff. I had not a suspicion the whole time that Turkey was in love with her. We seldom went into her grandmother's cottage, for she did not make us welcome. After we had taken Elsie home we generally went to visit Turkey's mother, with whom we were sure of a kind reception.

She was a patient, diligent woman, who looked as if she were nearly done with life and had only to gather up the crumbs of it. I have often wondered since what was her deepest thought—whether she was content to be unhappy, or whether she lived in hope of some blessedness beyond. It is marvelous with how little happiness some people can get through the world. Surely they are inwardly sustained with something even better than joy.

"Did you ever hear my mother sing?" asked Turkey as we sat together around her little fire on one of these occasions.

"No. I should like to very much," I answered.

The room was lighted only by a little oil lamp, though there was no blame to the fire of peats and dried oak bark.

"She sings such peculiar ballads as you never heard," said Turkey. "Do give us one, Mother."

She yielded, and in a low chanting voice, sang something like this:

Up cam' the waves o' the tide wi' a whush,
And back gaed the pebbles wi' a whurr,
Whan the king's ae son cam' walking i' the hush,
To hear the sea murmur and murr.

The half mune was risin' the waves abune,
An' a glimmer o cauld weet licht
Cam' ower the water straucht frae the mune,
Like a path across the nicht.

What's that, an' that, far oot i' the gray
Atwixt the mune and the land?
It's the bonny sea-maidens at their play—
Haud awa', king's son, frae the strand.

Ae rock stud up wi' a shadow at its foot:
The king's son stepped behind;
The merry sea-maidens cam' gambolling oot,
Combin' their hair i' the wind.

O merry their laugh when they felt the land
Under their light cool feet!
Each laid her comb on the yellow sand,
And the gladsome dance grew fleet.

But the fairest she laid her comb by itsel'
On the rock where the king's son lay.
He stole about, and the carven shell
He hid in his bosom away.

And he watched the dance till the clouds did gloom
And the wind blew an angry tune:
One after one she caught up her comb,
To the sea went dancin' doon.

But the fairest, wi' hair like the mune in a clud,
She sought till she was the last.
He creepin' went and watchin' stud,

And he thought to hold her fast.

She dropped at his feet without motion or heed;
He took her, and home he sped.—
All day she lay like a withered sea-weed,
On a purple and gowden bed.

But at night whan the wind frae the watery bars
Blew into the dusky room,
She opened her een like twa settin' stars,
And back came her twilight bloom.

The king's son knelt beside her bed:
She was his ere a month had passed;
And the cold sea-maiden he had wed
Grew a tender wife at last.

And all went well till her baby was born,
And then she couldna sleep;
She would rise and wander till breakin' morn,
Hark-harkin' the sound o' the deep.

One night when the wind was wailing about,
And the sea was speckled wi' foam,
From room to room she went in and out
And she came on her carven comb.

She twisted her hair with eager hands,
She put in the comb with glee:
She's out and she's over the glittering sands,
And away to the moaning sea.

One cry came back from far away:
He woke, and was all alone.
Her night robe lay on the marble gray,
And the cold sea-maiden was gone.

Ever and aye frae first peep o' the moon,
Whan the wind blew aff o' the sea,
The desert shore still up and doon
Heavy at heart paced he.

But never more came the maidens to play
From the merry cold-hearted sea;
He heard their laughter far out and away,
But heavy at heart paced he.

The next evening I looked for Elsie as usual, but she was not there. I went through my duties wondering about her, and could see that Turkey was anxious too. The moment school was over, we hurried away, almost without a word, to the cottage. There we found her weeping.

Her grandmother had died suddenly. She clung to Turkey, and seemed almost unaware of my presence. But I thought nothing of that. Had I been in her place, I too should have clung to Turkey from faith in his help and superior wisdom.

There were two or three old women in the place. Turkey went and spoke to them, and then took Elsie home to his mother. Jamie was asleep and they would not wake him.

How it was arranged, I forget, but both Elsie and Jamie lived for the rest of the winter with Turkey's mother. The cottage was rented out, and the cow taken home by their father. Before summer Jamie had got a place in a shop in the village, and then Elsie went back to be with her mother.

CHAPTER
THIRTY-NINE
—

AN EVENING VISIT

A s much as we could Turkey and I went to visit Elsie at her father's cottage. The evenings we spent there are among the happiest hours in my memory.

One evening in particular stands out as representative of the whole. I remember every point in the visit. I think it must have been almost the last.

We set out as the sun was going down on an evening in the end of April when the nightly frosts had not yet vanished. The hail was dancing about us as we started. The sun was disappearing in a bank of tawny orange clouds. The night would be cold and dark and stormy. But we cared nothing for that. A conflict with the elements always added to the pleasure of any undertaking then.

It was in the midst of a shower of hail, driven on the blasts of a keen wind, that we arrived at the little cottage. It had been built by Duff himself to receive his bride, and although since enlarged it was still a very little house. It had a foundation of stone, but the walls were of earthen turf. He had lined it with boards, however, and so made it warmer and more comfortable than most of the laborers' dwellings.

When we entered, a glowing fire of peat was in the fireplace, and the pot with the supper hung over it. Mrs. Duff was spinning, and Elsie, by the light of a little oil lamp suspended against the wall, was teaching her youngest brother to read, one arm around the little fellow who stood leaning against her, while the other pointed with a knitting needle to the letters of the spelling book that lay on her knee. The mother did not rise from her spinning, but spoke a kindly welcome, while Elsie got up, and without saying more than a word or two, set chairs for us by the fire and took the little fellow away to put him to bed.

"It's a cold night," said Mrs. Duff. "The wind seems to blow through me as I sit at my wheel. I wish my husband would come home."

"He'll be suppering his horses," said Turkey. "I'll just run across and give him a hand, and that'll bring him in all the sooner."

"Thank you, Turkey," said Mrs. Duff as he vanished.

"He's a fine lad," she remarked, much in the same phrase my father used when speaking of him.

"There's nobody like Turkey," I said.

"Indeed, I think you're right there, Ranald. I've never seen a better-behaved lad. He'll do something to distinguish himself some-day. I shouldn't wonder if he went to college, and wagged his head in a pulpit yet."

The idea of Turkey wagging his head in a pulpit made me laugh.

"Wait till you see," resumed Mrs. Duff, somewhat offended at my reception of her prophecy. "Folk will hear of him yet."

"I didn't mean he couldn't be a minister, Mrs. Duff. But I don't think he will take to that."

Here Elsie came back and lifted the lid of the pot to examine its contents. Then she began to set the white pine table in the middle of the floor, and by the time she had put the plates and spoons on it, the water in the pot was boiling, and she began to make the porridge. Just as it was ready, her father and Turkey came in. James Duff said grace, and we sat down to supper. The wind was blowing hard outside, and every now and then the hail came in deafening rattles against the little windows, and, descending the wide chim-ney, danced on the floor about the hearth. But not a thought of the long, stormy way between us and home interfered with the enjoy-ment of the hour.

After supper, which was enlivened by simple chat about the

crops and the doings on the farm, James turned to me.

"Haven't you got a song or ballad to give us, Ranald? I know you're always getting hold of such things."

I had expected this, for every time I went I tried to have something to read or repeat to them. As I could not sing, this was the nearest way I could contribute to the evening's entertainment. You must remember that there were very few books to be had then in that part of the country, and therefore any mode of literature was precious. The schoolmaster was the chief source from whom I derived my provision of this sort.

On this present occasion, I was prepared with a ballad of his. I remember every word of it now, and will give it to you, reminding you once more how easy it is to skip it if you do not care for that kind of thing.

"Bonny lassie, rosy lassie,
Ken ye what is care?
Had ye ever a thought, lassie,
Made yer hertie sair?"

Johnnie said it, Johnnie luikin'
Into Jeannie's face;
Seekin' in the garden hedge
For an open place.

"Na," said Jeannie, saftly smilin',
"Nought o' care ken I;
For they say the carlin'
Is better passit by."

"Licht o'hert ye are, Jeannie,
As o' foot and han'!
Lang be yours sic answer
To ony spierin' man."

"I ken what ye wad hae, sir,
Though yer words are few;
Ye wad hae me aye as careless,
Till I care for you."

"Dinna mock me, Jeannie, lassi

Wi'yer lauchin' ee;
For ye hae nae notion
What gaes on in me."

"No more I hae a notion
O' what's in yonder cairn;
I'm no sae pryin', Johnnie,
It's none o' my concern."

"Well, there's ae thing, Jeannie,
Ye canna help, my doo—
Ye canna help me carin'
Wi' a' my hert for you."

Johnnie turned and left her,
Listed for the war;
In a year cam' limpin;
Hame wi' mony a scar.

Wha was that was sittin;
Wan and worn wi' care?
Could it be his Jeannie
Aged and alter'd sair?

Her goon was black, her eelids
Reid wi' sorrow's dew:
Could she in a twalmonth
Be wife and widow too?

Jeannie's hert gaed wallop,
Ken't him whan he spak':
"I thocht that ye was deid, Johnnie.
Is't yersel' come back?"

"O Jeannie, are ye, tell me,
Wife or widow or baith?
To see ye lost as I am,
I wad be verra laith."

"I canna be a widow
That wife was never nane;

211

But gin ye will hae me,
Noo I will be ane."

His crutch he flang it frae him,
Forgetful o' war's harms;
But couldna stan' without it,
And fell in Jeannie's arms.

"That's not a bad ballad," said James Duff. "Have you a tune it would go to, Elsie?"

Elsie thought a little, and asked me to repeat the first verse. Then she sung it out clear and fair to a tune I had never heard before.

"That will do splendidly, Elsie," I said. "I will write it out for you, and then you will be able to sing the whole ballad the next time we come."

She made me no answer. She and Turkey were looking at each other, and she did not hear me. James Duff began to talk to me. Elsie was putting away the supper things.

In a few minutes I saw that she was gone, and so was Turkey. They were away some time. They did not return together, but first Turkey, and Elsie some minutes after. As the night was now getting quite stormy, James Duff suggested we return, and we obeyed. But neither Turkey nor I cared a straw for wind or hail.

I saw the Duffs at church most Sundays, but rarely spoke with Elsie. My father expected us to walk home with him. And generally I saw Turkey walk away with her.

CHAPTER
FORTY
—

A BREAK IN MY STORY

I am now rapidly approaching the moment at which I said I would bring this history to an end—namely, the moment when I became aware that my boyhood was behind me.

I left home that summer for the first time. I followed my brother Tom to the grammar school in the county town in order to make preparations to follow him to the University.

There was so much of novelty and expectation in the change that I did not feel the loneliness of separation from my father and the rest of my family much at first. That came afterward. For the time, the pleasure of a long ride on the top of the mail coach, with a bright sun and a pleasant breeze, the various incidents connected with changing horses and starting afresh, and then the first view of the sea—all of this occupied my attention too thoroughly.

I do not want to dwell on my experience at the grammar school. I worked fairly hard for the few months, and got on. How well I would do in the scholarship competition for the University remained doubtful. Before the time for the examination arrived, I went to spend a week at home. I had to return again to the city without once seeing Elsie, but it could not be helped. The Sunday of that week came on a stormy day late in October. Elsie was sick and unable to be in church, as Turkey informed me, and my father

214

had made so many other plans for me, with one thing and another, that I was not able to go out to see her.

Turkey was now doing a man's work on the farm, and stood as high as ever in the estimation of my father and everyone who knew him. He was a great favorite with Allister and Davie, and had taken the same place with them as he had earlier with me. I had lost nothing of my regard for him, and he talked to me with the same familiarity as before, urging me to diligence and thoroughness in my studies. "No one has ever done lasting work," he would say; "—that is, work that goes to the making of the world, without being in earnest as to the *what* and diligence as to the *how* of what he is doing."

"I don't want you to try to be a great man," he said once. "You might succeed, and then find out you had failed altogether."

"How could that be, Turkey?" I objected. "How can you succeed and fail both at once?"

"A man might succeed," he replied, "in doing what he wanted to do, and then find out that it was not in the least what he had thought it."

"What rule are you to follow then?" I asked.

"Just the rule of duty," he replied. "What you *ought* to do, that you must do. That is the essence of doing your duty—doing what you should do. Then when a choice comes in your life that *doesn't* involve duty, choose what you like best."

That is the substance of what he said. If anyone thinks it too preachy, I can only say that he would not have thought so if he had heard the words uttered in the homely forms and sounds of the Scottish tongue.

"Aren't you fit for something better than farm work yourself, Turkey?" I suggested to him.

"It's *my* work," he said in a decisive tone, "and work that I enjoy. Why should I not be content with it until something else presents itself?"

This conversation took place in the barn, where Turkey happened to be thrashing alone that morning. In turning the sheaf, or in laying a fresh one, there was always a moment's pause in the work, and it was at such times that we talked. So our conversation was a good deal broken.

I had buried myself in the straw, as in days of old, to keep myself warm, and there I lay and looked at Turkey while he thrashed, and thought to myself that his face had grown much more solemn than it used to be. But when he smiled, which was seldom, all the old merry sweetness dawned again. This was the last long talk I ever had with him.

The next day I returned for the examination. I gained a small scholarship, and then entered on my first winter at college.

My father wrote to me once a week or so, and occasionally I had a letter with more ink than substance in it from one of my younger brothers. Tom was now working in a lawyer's office in Edinburgh. I had no correspondence with Turkey. Mr. Wilson wrote to me sometimes, and along with good advice would occasionally send me some verses. But he told me little or nothing of what was going on.

CHAPTER

FORTY-ONE

―

THE END OF MY
BOYHOOD

It was a Saturday morning, very early in April of the following year, when I climbed aboard the mail coach to return to my home for the summer. The University year in Scotland is divided equally between winter and summer. And I had not completed my first full term.

The sky was bright, with great fleecy clouds sailing over it, from which now and then fell a shower in large drops. The wind was keen, and I had to wrap myself well in my cloak. But my heart was light and full of the pleasure of ending a successful labor, and the signs which sun and sky gave that the summer was at hand.

Five months had gone by since I last left home. It had seemed such an age to Davie that he burst out crying when he saw me. My father received me with a certain still tenderness, which seemed to grow upon him. Kirsty followed Davie's example, and Allister, without saying much, haunted me like my shadow. I saw nothing of Turkey that first evening home.

In the morning we went to church, of course, and I sat beside the reclining stone warrior, from whose face age had nearly worn the features away. I gazed at him all the time of the singing of the first psalm, and there grew upon me a strange solemnity, a sense of the passing away of earthly things, and a stronger conviction than I had ever had of the need of something that could not pass. This feeling lasted all the time of the service, and increased while I lingered in the church almost alone until my father came out of the vestry.

I stood in the passage, leaning against the tomb. A cloud came over the sun, and the whole church grew dark as a December day— gloomy and cheerless. I was aware of two old women talking close by me, but for some time paid no attention to what they said. They could not see me, for the pulpit was between them and me. But when I began to listen to them, I looked around and saw them.

"And when did it happen, you said?" asked one of them, whose head moved back and forth incessantly from palsy.

"About two o'clock this morning," answered the other, who leaned on a stick, almost bent double with rheumatism. "I had seen their next-door neighbor this morning, and he had seen Jamie, who goes home on Saturday nights, you know. But nobody's told the minister, and I'm just waiting to let him know, for she was a great favorite of his, and he's been to see her often. They're to be pitied— poor people! Nobody thought it would come so sudden like. When I saw her mother last, they had no notion it was so serious."

Before I could ask whom they were talking about, my father came up the aisle from the vestry and stopped to speak to the old women.

"Elsie Duff's gone, poor thing!" said the rheumatic one.

I immediately grew stupid with disbelief and grief. What followed I have forgotten. I heard more voices but could not comprehend them. When I came to myself I was alone in the church. I was standing beside the monument, leaning on the carved Crusader. The sun was again shining, and the old church was full of light. But the sunshine had changed to me, and I felt very mournful. I left the church hardly conscious of anything but a dull sense of loss.

I found my father very grave. He spoke tenderly of Elsie.

In the evening I went up to the farm to look for Turkey, who had not been at church morning or afternoon. I found him in one of the cowhouses, bedding the cows. His back was toward me when I entered.

"Turkey," I said.

He looked round with a slow mechanical motion, as if with a conscious effort of the will. His face was so white and wore such a look of loss that it almost terrified me like the presence of something awful.

I stood speechless. He looked at me for a moment, and then came slowly up to me and laid his hand on my shoulder.

"Ranald," he said, "we were to have been married next year."

Before the grief of the man, mighty in its silence, my whole being was humbled. Elsie had belonged to Turkey, and he had lost her, and his heart was breaking. I threw my arms round him and wept for him, not for myself. It was thus I ceased to be a boy.

Here, therefore, my story ends. Before I returned to the University the following fall, Turkey had enlisted in the army and left the place.

My father's half prophecy concerning him is now fulfilled. He is a general. I will not tell his name. For some reason or other he had taken his mother's, and by that he is well known.

I have never seen him or heard from him since he left my father's farm. But I am confident that if ever we meet, it will be as old and true friends.

BETHANY HOUSE PUBLISHERS
Minneapolis, Minnesota 55438

The Novels of George MacDonald Edited for Today's Reader

Edited Title	Original Title
The Fisherman's Lady	*Malcolm*
The Marquis' Secret	*The Marquis of Lossie*
The Baronet's Song	*Sir Gibbie*
The Shepherd's Castle	*Donal Grant*
The Tutor's First Love	*David Elginbrod*
The Musician's Quest	*Robert Falconer*
The Maiden's Bequest	*Alec Forbes*
The Curate's Awakening	*Thomas Wingfold*
The Lady's Confession	*Paul Faber*
The Baron's Apprenticeship	*There and Back*
The Highlander's Last Song	*What's Mine's Mine*
The Gentlewoman's Choice	*Weighed and Wanting*
The Laird's Inheritance	*Warlock O'Glenwarlock*
The Minister's Restoration	*Salted with Fire*
A Daughter's Devotion	*Mary Marston*
The Peasant Girl's Dream	*Heather and Snow*
The Landlady's Master	*The Elect Lady*
The Poet's Homecoming	*Home Again*

MacDonald Classics Edited for Young Readers

Wee Sir Gibbie of the Highlands
Alec Forbes and His Friend Annie
At the Back of the North Wind
The Adventures of Ranald Bannerman

George MacDonald: Scotland's Beloved Storyteller by Michael Phillips
Discovering the Character of God by George MacDonald
Knowing the Heart of God by George MacDonald
A Time to Grow by George MacDonald
A Time to Harvest by George MacDonald